Written in the Sand

PACIFIC SHORES
- BOOK 4 -

Written in the Sand

Brynn STEWART

PACIFIC SHORES SERIES
Contemporary Christian Romance

Beyond the Waves – BOOK ONE

Caught in the Current – BOOK TWO

Song of the Surf – BOOK THREE

Written in the Sand – BOOK FOUR

Other books by Brynn Stewart

THE RIVERSONG SERIES
Contemporary Christian Romance

Angel Kisses and Riversong – BOOK ONE

Soft Kisses and Birdsong – BOOK TWO

Butterfly Kisses and Windsong – BOOK THREE

HEARTS OF HOLLYWOOD
Contemporary Christian Romance Novellas

My Blue Havyn – BOOK ONE

Mistletoe and Mochas – BOOK TWO

Kittens and Snow Flurries – BOOK THREE

MISTY COVE
Contemporary Christian Romance Novellas

The Heart of Christmas – BOOK ONE

The Wonder of Christmas – BOOK TWO

Written in the Sand
PACIFIC SHORES, Book 4

Cover design by Lynnette Bonner of Indie Cover Design
images ©
   www.istock.com, File: # 479547069 – couple
   www.depositphotos.com, File: # 3954136 – sky

Author photo © Emily Hinderman, EMH Photography

Scripture taken from *The Message*. Copyright © 1993, 1994,
1995, 1996, 2000, 2001, 2002. Used by permission of NavPress
Publishing Group.

Scripture taken from THE HOLY BIBLE, NEW
INTERNATIONAL VERSION®, NIV® Copyright © 1973, 1978,
1984, 2011 by Biblica, Inc.® Used by permission. All rights
reserved worldwide.

ISBN: 978-1-942982-65-4

Printed in the U.S.A.

Jeremiah 29:11

"For I know the plans I have for you,"
declares the Lord,
"plans to prosper you and not to harm you,
plans to give you hope and a future."

Chapter 1

Riley Ross set her bags of groceries from the Thrift and Save into the back seat of her old Jeep and glanced at the time on her phone. She yanked open the driver's door.

Of course Mom couldn't have given her any more than five minutes' notice that she needed Rem picked up from soccer practice today, because that would be too much to ask.

From the slight slur in Mom's voice when she'd called, Riley would be willing to bet her last dollar Mom was keeping a barstool warm, and a healthy tab running, down at Pete's. And why was it Mom hadn't arranged to have Rem picked up in the first place? Mom couldn't even drive right now. But had she thought ahead to ask Roddy, their groundskeeper, to plan to get him? No.

Riley just hoped Mom had been telling the truth about taking a cab. *The last thing I need to deal with is Mom getting pulled over for driving under the influence.* Especially since her license was currently revoked from the last incident.

A huge sigh slipped free. This was the first day of soccer for Rem. And she supposed it was going to become her regular responsibility to pick him up each day. Because it was seemingly beyond Mom's capability to get her son to and from the places he needed to be when she was so busy helping gravity with its job of keeping the chaise lounge firmly on the floor at the house. Or instructing Lucia, the live-in maid, what meals to prepare and what rooms to clean. Or apparently equally taxing, keeping Pete in business.

Riley grimaced at herself in the rearview mirror as she pulled out onto the two-lane coastal highway in front of the grocery store and headed toward the high school. "Stop it." She gave herself a pointed look.

It was too easy to let her frustrations with her mother's behavior make her forget that it was all a mask to bury the pain Mom refused to face. Heaven knew Riley had tried to get her to counseling on more than one occasion. And had talked to her about moving on until she was blue in the face.

Jesus, it's going to take something big to reach her, I'm afraid.

Thankfully, Riley's job as a second-grade teacher's aide had regular hours. She got off at four o'clock each day. So it wouldn't be too much of a hardship to swing by the high school and pick up Rem and run him up to the Bluffs. She reminded herself how thankful she'd been when she heard he'd decided to play soccer. She hoped it would keep him from finding too much trouble this year. The way Rem was always trying to prove himself to everyone had her just a little bit terrified of what he might get involved in during this his first year in high school. She'd heard the school had hired a new coach. Hopefully, he would be a guy who had his head on straight and not one of those macho jerks who would teach his kids to obliterate the opponents no matter what.

The late August sun beat down unmercifully and Riley could feel sweat dampening the armpits of her light blue silk top. She lowered all four windows and let the breeze cool the interior of the car. At least her hair was up in a bun off her neck today, not that the wind was probably doing her any favors in that department. But the only thing on her schedule for tonight, after dropping Rem at home, was to change into jeans and head over to finish up some of the remodeling to the house on Second Street, so it wasn't like it mattered what she looked like.

She whipped into the high school parking lot and stopped in a slot close to the soccer field. She could see the team doing cool down stretches near the far goal, but couldn't pick out who Rem's coach might be from this distance.

She propped her elbow against the window and rested her head against her fist. Her eyes slid closed. Five a.m. had been a long time ago. And she still had a lot of work left in her day. Maybe she could catch a few minutes of rest while she waited.

Birds twittered lustily from the shade of the maple off to her left, and somewhere high overhead she heard the shrill cry of a gull. The sun beat down on her head warming her and only increasing her drowsiness. An insect droned by and the wind slipped through grasses and leaves, whispering tranquility and peace. All the details blurred into a soft haze.

Riley's head fell off her fist and jolted her awake. She blinked and focused. The team was standing now and several players were already near her in the parking lot loading their sports bags into vehicles and laughing and joking with one another.

She scanned the field for Remington, but didn't see him anywhere. He might be expecting Mom to pick him up from the parking lot on the other side of the pitch. Riley sighed and rolled up her windows, then climbed from the Jeep and slung her purse over one shoulder as she clicked the locks into place. She should have thought to ask Mom if they'd predetermined a place to meet. Not that Mom would have necessarily remembered if they had.

She rubbed the back of her neck, willing away the last vestiges of sleepiness as she picked her way up the low grassy hill to the level of the field.

She sheltered her eyes with one hand as she scanned the players, searching for Rem's red mop of curls. Finally, she spotted him, still in the center of the field twirling a soccer ball around with his feet while he apparently engaged in a conversation with...

Riley froze where she stood. She felt the heels of her pumps sink into the soft moist soil at the edge of the field, but couldn't seem to move. Her hands fluttered to her hair and she could feel even without the aid of a mirror that the disarray would be hopeless to repair.

She sighed. Her mouth was dry. And all thoughts of sleepiness fled. In fact, her heart was beating so hard anyone might have thought she'd just been running a 5K instead of napping in her Jeep.

And all because of the sight of the man talking to Rem. The man with the whistle hanging around his neck. The man who was quite obviously the new soccer coach at Marinville High.

Jalen Rivera.

She shook the surprise away and focused on the simple happiness washing through her, instead. Jalen was the reason she'd finally seen the Truth that God loved her and wanted her to serve Him. The reason she was serving Him today. And without Jesus to lean on over the past few years, she didn't know where she would be right now. She thought back to what her life had been like not long before she met Jalen for the first time, and shuddered. Thankfully, God had helped her put those memories behind her little by little over the last couple years. And that had all started because of Jalen – well, Marie and Dakota and Taysia had a big part in her salvation story too.

She couldn't be happier that Rem was going to have such a great coach. She just totally hadn't expected to see him here. Or her reaction to seeing him here.

Slowly, she eased her heels from the dirt and started toward them.

Her thoughts turned to the past and the promise she'd made herself. The night Nate had beaten her so badly she'd lost their baby, he'd left the house in a drunken rage and wrapped himself around a rock along the Pacific Highway and killed himself. After that night, she'd promised herself she would never be so vulnerable to the power of loving a man again.

And then she'd met Jalen. He'd only been in town for a short time for Reece and Marie Cahill's wedding, but Riley had felt more of a connection with him in that short time she'd known him than she ever had with any man previously. But he'd had to go back to his job on the other side of the state.

Jalen had texted with her for a few months after he'd returned home, but then, to sever ties with some of her old friends who were not such great influences, Riley had changed carriers and her number. She'd thought about reinitiating contact numerous times, but her newfound commitment to remain single had always kept her from doing so.

Now she took a breath. It was great to see him again, but she needed to keep up her guard.

Because if ever there was a man who could

tempt her to give up her vow, it was Jalen Rivera. And...her hand skimmed over her abdomen... For his sake it was best she remember that and keep her distance.

Jalen bent and grabbed up his towel from the bag near his feet and scrubbed at the sweat coating his forehead and hair as he smiled at Remington Ross. The kid had shot up quite a few inches since the last time Jalen had seen him two years ago, when he'd been in town for Reece Cahill's wedding. He was still scrawny as all get out, and short for his age, but that didn't bother Jalen in the least. The kid could control the ball like few his age, and from what he'd seen today, Rem had a good understanding of the positions of the game. And it was obvious his interest went beyond just an understanding to an actual love for the sport, as evidenced by the fact that while most of the team had already meandered off the field, Remington was still here pacing through some footwork.

Jalen slung his towel over his shoulder and rested one hand on the kid's shoulder. "Nice job out here today. You have a real knack for the game."

What he really wanted to talk about was Remington's older sister. The woman who was the reason he'd come back to Marinville in the first place. Was she faring better now that some time had passed after the death of her abusive boyfriend? Was she seeing anyone? Jalen scooped up his sports bag. Please, heaven forbid, she wasn't married was she? But he held all those questions inside. Time would reveal the answers. Time would tell him whether he was simply a fool lingering over memories of a woman who had somehow captured his heart in a few short days, or whether something could actually come of it.

Remington bent and picked up his ball, resting it against one hip as he eyed Jalen. The expression in his eyes said he wasn't quite sure whether to take Jalen's compliments seriously.

Jalen nodded. "I mean it. I was impressed with what I saw today. But I hope you won't let that go to your head because the whole team has some improving to do."

Remington shrugged. "Sure. I get ya."

"Good. So I'll catch you tomorrow, okay?" He waved goodbye and turned to head for his car in the parking lot. He stilled, his heart rate kicking up as though he hadn't just spent the last fifteen minutes cooling down.

Picking her way toward them from the edge of the field, one small hand shading her eyes, was Riley. Black slacks. A silvery blue blouse. Red hair piled into a messy knot at the back of her head. And – he swallowed – looking even more beautiful than he remembered.

Take a breath, Rivera. He did that, and then forced one foot in front of the other in what he hoped looked to be a casual stroll across the field and not something similar to the dashing, dancing, and leaping of joy his heart was doing in his chest.

He stopped a few feet before her when he suddenly realized he probably smelled like a field horse after a long day of plowing. He resisted a grimace. Good thing the breeze was brisk so the odors wouldn't linger around. "Riley." He offered her a smile.

"J-Jalen." Her face looked stricken, but she followed up quickly with "It's so good to see you again!" She stepped toward him, intent on pulling him into a welcoming embrace.

He jumped back. "It's good to see you too, but I probably smell like the wrong end of a mule right about now." He nearly clenched his eyes shut. *Talk about smooth, Rivera. Way to leave her with such a charming picture.*

"Of course." She offered the reassurance, but her tone said she thought she'd somehow offended him. "I'm sorry, I didn't mean to—" Her gaze searched out his left hand where it still gripped the towel slung over his shoulder and she stuttered to a stop and let the rest of the sentence trail away, then dropped her gaze to the grass at their feet.

His own gaze searched out her left hand where she twirled her car keys nervously. No ring, at least.

A herd of wild mustangs on the run must have taken up residence in his chest. When she'd cut off contact with him, he'd been discouraged. But he'd decided to honor her obvious wishes. But something about this woman wouldn't release his thoughts and he didn't think a day had gone by that he hadn't wondered how she was doing. He'd weaseled information out of Dakota a few times, but it had never been enough. So, for two years he'd been waiting and praying. Wanting to come back and pursue Riley, but never feeling it was quite the right time.

And then he'd seen the ad for the high school soccer coach—or rather Dakota had sent it to him in an email with a little winking face and no other comments. The email had arrived the day after he and Justus had learned that the funding for their ministry, Deschutes Rejuvenation, had dried up and the church that had been sponsoring the program was cutting it. He had a feeling that cutback had answered a few of Justus's prayers as well as his own. They both had been willing to continue serving, but both of them had been serving with divided hearts for the past couple years.

The breeze tugged at the golden-red strands of Riley's hair and he noticed that the sun had brought out a few light freckles across the bridge of her nose. Seeing her again made him feel like an out-of-oxygen scuba diver breaking through the surface of the water and pulling in that first life-giving breath of air.

"So you're here to pick up Rem—"

"—So you're the new soccer coach."

They spoke at the same time, and then smiled at each other sheepishly.

She tilted her head. "I hadn't heard you were back in town?"

There was something different, *less vulnerable*,

about her countenance. "I just got here last night. They interviewed me on Skype since the last term at Deschutes Rejuvenation was still going."

"Dakota told me your funding was cut. I'm sorry about that."

He shrugged. His years in that ministry had been good. Blessed. But there wasn't a place he would rather be right now than where he was standing. "Was time to move on, I guess."

She spun her keys around one finger. "Where are you staying?"

"Reece has given Justus and me a room at a discount out at Serenity Shores Bed and Breakfast, for now. But we're looking for a place to rent."

"I see. Well, I can tell you I'm very pleased that you'll be Rem's soccer coach."

She tilted her head and smiled fondly at him, but it was a smile that suddenly had him second-guessing his plan to make his feelings known to her, because the gesture was sisterly. Cordial. Platonic. Guarded.

She tucked a wisp of hair behind her ear. "I'd better get going. It's nice to see you again, Jalen." She looked past him. "Rem, Mom asked me to pick you up. Let's go, please."

"Just a sec!" Remington called back, continuing to dribble the ball toward the soccer goal at the far end of the field.

Riley opened her mouth to call him again, but her phone rang and she paused to dig it out of her purse. She glanced at the caller ID, a small frown forming on her brow.

He should go and leave her to her call in private, but after seeing her for the first time in two years, he wasn't quite ready to deprive himself again so soon. Especially since this might be the most interaction he'd ever get with her.

She pressed on her screen. "Hi, Kylen, what's up?" The furrows on her brow deepened as she listened. "I'm at the school picking up Rem from soccer practice, why?" Her hand went to her forehead. "She what?" Her eyes fell closed. "Was anyone hurt?" A breath left her in a long, slow exhale. "Well, thank God for that. I'll get Rem and...we'll be down in a few minutes, I guess." She blinked hard. Then blinked again. "No, don't be sorry. This is not your fault. We'll be there as soon as we can." She hung up and stood staring at her phone for a long moment, as though she wished she could go back a few minutes in time and not answer it.

He shouldn't intrude, but he went against his better judgment and asked, "Everything alright?"

She looked up as though coming back from someplace far away. "Uh...no, but thanks for asking." She stretched her lips, but it didn't come across like much of a smile.

He reached out and squeezed her shoulder before he thought better of it. Then snatched his hand away. He tipped his head toward the boy still practicing shots into the net. "I'll get him for you." Turning, he jogged toward Remington, wondering what news Kylen, one of Marinville's four police officers, would have been calling her about. Jalen knew her father had left the family to move in with his secretary in another city a couple years ago, and her mother hadn't been doing well even before that. *Lord, whatever it is, give her the strength to make it through. Let me help her through it, if I can.*

Chapter 2

Riley's hands trembled as she drove toward the police station. Her whole body trembled.

This would be Mom's third DUI in the past two years. The third since Dad left. And she likely wasn't going to get off easy this time.

So many emotions pressed for preeminence, Riley's mind couldn't seem to pick one to settle on. Anger over her mother's irresponsibility. Sorrow for all Mom would now have to face. Fear for what this was going to do to Rem. But most of all, anxiety over how she was going to take care of him because Mom was surely going to be in jail for awhile.

Her mind flashed to her father. The last two times Mom had been arrested he'd been out of the country on business, so she'd taken full responsibility for Rem. But this time would be considerably longer, she felt sure.

Rem was staring into his lap, hands clenched. Her heart went out to her brother. No kid should have to deal with things like this. His palpable silence was telling.

She pulled into a slot at the police station and shut off the engine.

Remington didn't move.

She didn't move.

She closed her eyes. *Lord...?* Silence was her only answer.

Rem shuffled around in his seat. "She's going to be alright, isn't she?"

Riley forced herself into action and pulled open her door. "I'm sure she will be, Rem. Let's just go in and find out what the next steps will be, okay?" How did the lie slip so easily off her tongue? Everything was certainly not going to be alright for a woman who'd been driving under the influence, especially since she wasn't even supposed to be behind the wheel!

Officer Kylen Sumner met them at the door as they entered the precinct. He held out his hand with a nod, but didn't say it was good to see her. His expression showed compassion, but also grim reality. "Right this way." He ushered them into a quiet room with stark walls and a table in the middle. Plastic chairs encircled the table. "Please have a seat."

Riley felt robotic as she sank into the chair and placed her purse on the floor beside her. Remington plopped into the seat next to her, equally quiet.

Kylen's brows lifted as he eased into the seat across from them. "First, I want to say as your friend, Riley, I'm really sorry about all this."

Don't be kind, Kylen. Just give it to me. Since he was married to Taysia, one of her best friends, they saw a lot of each other. She bit the inside of her lip. He was only trying to be nice. "Yeah. Thanks."

He got right down to business then. "I need to ask you both a few questions, if that's okay?"

"Sure." Riley nodded.

Kylen's gaze darted between them, then settled on Remington. "When's the last time you spoke with your mom?"

Brushing back his sweat-dampened mop of red hair, Rem shrugged. "Last night at dinner."

"You didn't see her this morning?"

Rem shook his head. "She was still sleeping when I left to catch the bus for school."

Riley swallowed down her resentment toward Mom for leaving Rem to fend for himself so much.

Kylen jotted a couple notes and then stood holding out a hand to Rem. "Thanks, Rem. I need to talk to your sister for a bit and I need you to wait out in the waiting area. Officer O'Keefe here will show you where to go."

Remington stiffened. "I'm not a little kid. I can deal with whatever."

Kylen's gaze swung to her.

She was torn for only a moment before she decided to let him stay. They both would have to deal with the consequences of Mom's choices. He might as well not hear the details secondhand.

She nodded. "I think it's fine for him to stay."

Kylen sighed, waved away the younger officer,

and settled back into his seat. He glanced through his notes and then up at her.

"And you? When was the last time you spoke to her?"

Riley rubbed her forehead with a sigh. "She called me from Pete's at about five minutes to five this evening and asked me to pick Rem up from soccer practice. I asked her if she'd taken a cab and she assured me she had. I take it she was driving her car when she crashed?"

Kylen swallowed. "Yes. And there's more. She did considerable damage to the front of Thrift and Save."

"Thrift and Save?" Riley frowned. "Why was she there?"

Kylen shook his head. "We don't know and she didn't seem to want to say." He eased back in his chair and folded his arms. "Conjecture is she might have been trying to" —he hesitated, cleared his throat, glanced down, then bounced a compassionate glance between them—"kill herself."

"What?!" Riley's word was barely audible for all the shock it contained.

Remington slumped back in his seat.

Riley reached over and grabbed his hand.

Kylen continued. "She drove full speed across the parking lot and into the brick wall. Wasn't wearing a seatbelt."

Riley planted her forehead into one palm. "Is she hurt?"

"She's pretty banged up, but she was checked

out by paramedics on the scene and by a doctor as soon as she arrived at the hospital, and she seems to just have surface cuts and abrasions, a broken nose, and a cracked rib."

"So she's at the hospital now?"

Kylen nodded. "But I'm afraid she's under arrest and," his gaze flickered to Rem, "Judge Mason has ruled she can't have any visitors at this time."

Riley wasn't surprised by that. Remington had smuggled Mom a bottle of whiskey the last time she'd ended up in the hospital with a DUI. "Okay, we understand." A wave of weariness washed over Riley. How was she going to deal with all this? "Do you need anything else from us?"

"Not right now." Kylen stood. "Her hearing will be on Monday at eleven o'clock, but Riley," he paused with his hand on the door, "it's not looking good for bail. I don't think she's going to get it easy this time."

Riley pressed her lips together and retrieved her purse. "Thanks, Kylen." She squeezed Rem around the shoulders. "Come on, I'll take you home."

Riley swung by her house and packed a small bag. She left a note for her roommate, Dakota, that she'd be living with Rem for a while and set it in the middle of the dining room table, and then they were on their way. She tried Dad three times, and finally left him a voice mail.

The week settled into a routine fairly quickly after that. Lucia was on vacation and wouldn't be back until the following Monday, so Riley would rise and make breakfast, get Rem on the bus to the high school and then quickly finish her own preparations and head off to work. After she got off work she spent the few minutes she had before needing to get Rem from soccer either running to the grocery store or doing a little of the remodeling she still needed to finish to the house on Second. After getting Rem from practice, she took him home and got him settled, then headed back to town to continue the remodeling work. The only incident all week had happened last night when she'd had to take his cell phone away because at midnight he was still up texting his friends. Hopefully, she wouldn't have to fight that battle again after she gave him back his phone tonight.

Thankfully, it was Friday. And tonight she just needed to finish putting the second coat of paint on the last bedroom and tack up the chair rail she'd already measured and cut. Then tomorrow...blessed sleep.

Remington hadn't lingered after practice any more since that first day. He always came straight to the Jeep and so, despite the fact that she'd often wondered how Jalen was settling in, she hadn't bumped into him again.

But now as she sat waiting, she realized that all the other kids had cleared out of the parking lot and Remington should have arrived already.

All week long Rem had spoken nothing but praise for Coach Rivera, and yesterday he'd told her, with a sparkle in his eyes, that he might get to start at right forward if he could improve his shot a little. Rem was probably staying after for a bit today to do some more practice shots on the goal, but they needed to get going. She'd promised her agent the house would be ready to show to a couple tomorrow, and she was anxious to get the finishing touches done.

She couldn't see the end of the field from where she was parked because of the maintenance shed. Wearily, she climbed from the Jeep and went in search of Remington.

But when she rounded the corner of the groundskeeper's building, Jalen was coming toward her in a T-shirt and soccer shorts. He paused as though surprised to see her, and then a strange look crossed his face.

"What?" She folded her arms against the betrayal of her heart which leapt in ecstasy at the sight of him.

"Please don't tell me Rem is quitting the team?"

She shook her head and then gestured up toward the field. "I was just going up to get him."

Jalen frowned and tugged on the strap of the sports bag slung over one broad shoulder. "He didn't show up for practice today."

"He didn't?" Riley's weariness threatened to spill over into tears. She pressed one hand to her forehead and spun away from the man, trying to think where Rem might have gone instead. He loved soccer. She couldn't imagine him choosing to miss practice. Where should she start looking? The school office would be closed by now, and she didn't know who any of his close friends were.

Jalen stepped up beside her, watching her closely with those soft brown eyes of his. "One of the boys, Keith, said he saw him at lunch, but he wasn't at any of the afternoon classes they shared. I thought he might have gone home sick."

"Keith Tuppins?"

Jalen nodded.

"Well that's a place to start, I guess. Thanks. And sorry he wasn't at practice." She turned for her Jeep before she did something stupid like throw herself into his arms and ask him to take all her troubles away.

But he spoke from behind her. "Riley, can you try and call him?"

She shook her head. "I have his phone."

"I see. Well, if you don't mind, I'd like to come along?"

She hesitated.

"Might make the guys a little more forthcoming."

That was true. And the thought of having someone by her side while she hunted down her wayward brother was more than a little comforting. Might keep her from killing him once she found him, too.

"Sure." She motioned him toward the passenger side of her Jeep.

They rode to Keith's in silence, but somehow she and Jalen had always had an easy connection between them and the quiet didn't feel awkward.

When she knocked on the door at the Tuppins' place and asked to speak to Keith her stomach was knotted up tighter than a boxer's fist.

Keith came to the door looking uncertain, but his eyes brightened when they landed on Jalen. "Oh, hi Coach."

Jalen nodded at him but let her do the talking for which she was thankful. "Keith, Jal—uh, Coach Rivera said you mentioned at practice that you saw Rem at lunch but then he didn't come to any of his afternoon classes? Do you know where he might have gone?"

The boy's face lost a shade of color and then another. He glanced back and forth from Jalen to her as if he'd like to slam the door in her face but didn't want to do it in front of his coach.

Jalen spoke for the first time. "It's okay, Keith. Rem was supposed to be at practice and his sister is just worried about him and needs to make sure he's safe. Please tell us what you know."

Keith shuffled his feet. "He went with some of the guys to a party."

Riley was at once relieved to know it was just a stupid decision he'd made and horrified that he'd chosen to go to a party instead of school and soccer.

"Where at?" Even she heard the resigned exhaustion in her tone.

Keith glanced at the welcome mat beneath her feet. "I don't know the exact place, but it's...in Portland."

"Portland!? That's over two hours from here!"

Keith nodded.

"Do you know anyone who knows where they were going?"

Keith shook his head. "Only word I heard was it was going to be fun and anyone who wanted to go should meet Tony Cruz in the parking lot after lunch. He was driving."

Tony Cruz. Riley felt the blood retreat from her head. Of course Rem wouldn't be going to a party in Portland with someone nice. No. He had to run off with a kid who'd been in the local news just last week for spray painting curse words on the back wall of the elementary school. The elementary's video surveillance had caught him. She herself had spent some time with the other teachers scrubbing it off before the kids arrived for school.

Her hands clenched and she felt her blood pressure begin to rise.

Jalen's hand settled at her back. "Thanks Keith. Good practice today. See you Monday." Jalen gently propelled her toward her Jeep. "Come on. Want me to drive?"

She gave him the keys without hesitation. She was so angry right now she would be in danger of getting a speeding ticket or even worse, killing herself and Jalen if she got behind the wheel.

Jalen backed out of the drive and started down the road, then looked over at her. "Where are we going?"

She waved a hand. "Back to your car at the

school, I guess. There's no way I can run off to Portland and expect to find him. I'll just have to wait to kill him till he gets back home."

Jalen gave a wry chuckle then tossed her a repentant look. "Sorry. I don't mean to laugh, but I so know how you are feeling right now."

Riley sighed and propped her head against her fist. Yeah, he probably did since he'd spent the last ten years working with troubled boys. "And here I'd thought the week was going so great. This is his payback for me taking his phone last night."

Sympathy touched Jalen's expression. "We could try finding Tony Cruz's number? Calling him to find out where they are? I'd go with you to Portland, if you want?"

Riley's hopes momentarily surged. "That's a good idea." She dug for her phone in her purse and dialed 411. But there was no listing for a Tony Cruz, Anthony Cruz, or Antonio Cruz living in Marinville. She dropped her hand back to her lap in defeat. "No luck."

"Maybe Rem has Tony's number in his phone?"

She shook her head. "I thought of that but Rem has a password on his phone and I don't know it." She rubbed at the ache in her forehead. "I guess I'll just have to pray and trust him to God."

"Sometimes entrusting them to God is one of the hardest things we have to do." Jalen reached over and squeezed her hand.

Her heart skipped a beat and she pulled her hand from his on the pretext of putting her phone back in her purse. This man could so easily make her forget all her reasons why it would be best never to get into another relationship again.

Jalen apparently took the hint because he settled his palm against the stick shift, giving her space. "So when is your mom's first day in court?"

She sighed. Yet one more thing to worry about. "Monday. And I don't think she'll be getting out on bail."

"And custody for Remington? What's happening with that?"

Riley squeezed the muscles at the base of her neck. "I've left messages for my dad three times this week and he hasn't returned my calls. So I will have to take custody of him, I guess. Dad pays Mom enough alimony to keep the house going and provide for her and Rem. Hopefully he'll...I don't know. I guess if he quits paying it, I'll just have to let Lucia and Roddy go and have Rem move into the house with Dakota and me." She could do it. She might have to break down and use some of Dad's money from her account to support Rem, but that wasn't the same as using it for herself. Tears threatened and she blinked hard to keep them at bay, turning her face toward her window so Jalen wouldn't see.

They drove in silence until her phone rang and she scrambled to snatch it up. It was an unfamiliar number. *Please let this be Rem, God.* "Hello?"

"Riley?"

"Remington Dylan Ross! Where are you?"

"I know, look, just relax, alright? I'm headed back to Marinville now. I caught a ride with a guy and he let me use his phone."

"You caught a ride with someone? Who?"

"I don't know." She could almost hear his signature shrug. "Just some guy who picked me up when I was thumbing for a ride."

"Remington Ross! You were hitchhiking?! Do you know how many crazies are out there?"

"Just chill, Ri. I felt bad that I left without telling you. Now I'm coming home. Just thought you'd like to know." He ended with a mild curse.

"Well, if he doesn't kill you, I'm going to do it when you get home!"

Jalen reached over and laid his hand on her arm. His look said "take a breath."

She pinched the bridge of her nose. "I'm sorry. Rem, I'm sorry. I didn't mean it. I'm just so relieved you are alright. Can he bring you all the way to Marinville?"

Rem exchanged a few muffled words with the driver, and then came back on the line. "Yeah. He says he can drop me at the Thrift and Save."

"Okay, give me a call when you get to the edge of town and I'll meet you over there."

"Okay. Bye, Ri." The phone clicked off in her ear and she dropped it into her lap with a relieved sigh. Now her only worry was whether he'd been picked up by a serial murderer.

"He alright?"

"For now." Riley nodded.

"He's a good kid, Riley. I see a lot of changes in him from two years ago."

She rolled her eyes but said, "Yeah, thanks." A puff of pent-up tension she didn't know she'd been holding shot from her lungs. She had been trying to be a good influence on him. She took him to church with her whenever she could talk him into it. And he'd even gone to the Bible camp she'd paid for last summer.

She lost the battle she'd been waging and the tears spilled over, but she kept her face averted and swiped quietly at the betraying wetness. The last thing Jalen probably wanted was an emotional female basket case on his hands.

By the time the school came into view, she had herself in hand once more and her eyes were dry. Still, when Jalen parked next to his rig and she came around the Jeep to get her keys from him, she kept her face averted. "Thanks for coming with me, Jalen. I appreciate it." She reached out one hand for her keys, still not looking at him.

"Ri? He's going to be okay. Anyone who wanted to harm him wouldn't have let him use their phone." He touched her chin and bent down, drawing her gaze to his. His expression softened and he tilted his head, taking in what she could only assume were her red rimmed eyes. "He'll be okay." His hand slid up to rest against the side of her face. And his thumb stroked soft caresses against her cheek. He didn't offer any other words, but just his closeness was comfort.

Riley knew she should pull away, but everything in her drew her to the support and care he offered. He had her full attention and she couldn't find the strength to retreat.

The brown of his eyes was dark chocolate drizzled with caramel highlights. One eyebrow had a tiny scar through it, and the dark stubble coating his jaw only accentuated the angular masculinity of his face. His lower lip was full, his upper one slightly thinner with a distinct dip in the center. She wondered what it would feel like to have those lips against her own, and her mouth went dry. Heat seared through her and she stepped back, forcing her gaze to the side of her Jeep.

Jalen was offering nothing more than consolation and comfort after a long trying week, and she shouldn't even be contemplating kisses when her little brother could still be in danger, even if it was probably true that Rem would be fine.

Jalen swiped his cheek against one shoulder and settled his hands against his hips. His eyes narrowed, honing in on her. "Where are you going tonight?"

She worked the weary muscles at the back of her neck. "I have some remodeling to finish on a house I've been working on."

"Let me come help you? You shouldn't be alone right now."

"No no. It's fine. I'm sure you're tired after a long day."

"And you're not?"

She offered a weary smile of acknowledgement. "I'll be fine."

"You'll be better if you let me come help you." He grinned charmingly.

"Jalen...isn't there some woman somewhere waiting in anticipation to spend the evening with you?"

His grin broadened. "A guy could hope." He tilted her a look. "I'm trying to get her to say yes to me right now."

She laughed and couldn't deny that her heart soared to learn he wasn't connected to anyone else.

She also couldn't resist a flirtatious retort. "Fine, but only if you buy me Chinese takeout on the way."

She bit her lip. Weston Hollingsworth had been asking her out for over a year now and she'd staunchly resisted him every time. How had Jalen elicited a "yes" the first time he asked to spend an evening with her?

His brows lifted. "The lady drives a hard bargain, I see."

She was in with both feet now so she offered a teasing wince. "Too much to ask?"

All humor seeped out of his expression. "Not at all." His gaze roamed her face, pausing on her lips before rebounding to her eyes. "I'll even throw in dessert."

She snatched her keys from him, yanked open her Jeep door, and scuttled inside before she could be tempted to ask what type of dessert he meant.

"Follow me then," she said, just before she slammed the door and started her engine to drown out his knowing chuckles.

Chapter 3

Once they were at the little house on Second with their bag of Chinese takeout, Riley dug out a couple paper plates and plastic cups. She was here often enough that she'd left a supply of things like that to have on hand.

Jalen stepped into the kitchen and set his sports bag in one corner as he took in the freshly remodeled room. "Wow, I like it. Did you do this yourself?"

Riley glanced around the space. She'd painted the walls a deep red and the cupboards stark white. She'd replaced the doors on a couple of the cupboards with glass ones, and added decorative shelving to the interior. She'd already added some red dishes she'd found at the thrift store in Portland to the cupboards as display items. The stainless steel sink gleamed from where it was set into the shiny black granite countertop. The appliances were new, but had a retro look and were deep red to match the walls. Near the bay window was an old fashioned corner booth with bright red buttoned-leather cushioning.

She placed the paper plates on the small Formica and chrome table that nestled into the corner booth. "Yeah, I had fun with this one, except for that red paint. It took three coats to get good coverage."

"This is amazing, Riley." Admiration shone in his expression. He trailed one hand over the stainless faucet. "Are you doing this for yourself?"

She shook her head and took her time pulling two cream sodas from the interior of the fridge so she could compose her features. She would love to remodel a little place like this for herself. But when her father had kicked her out of the house the year she turned eighteen, she'd made herself a promise. Even though he'd generously supplied a bank account for her, she wouldn't spend one red cent of his guilt-assuaging gift on herself. She grasped the cans in one hand and turned back toward the booth. It was likely the red color that triggered the memory and sent one hand to trace the scar just behind her ear in her hairline.

There had been a year when Mom had gone for reds in one of her many remodels – deep crimson walls, a red velvet bedding set, red glass lamps, and cream accents like the polar bear fleece on the floor.

Katherine, you're a whore! Who's the father?

You are! Dylan, I swear!

The whimper her mother loosed pierced Riley clean through because she knew Mommy was trying to be quiet and not wake her. Still, she'd peered around the corner, Mr. Griz, her stuffed bear, tucked safely under one arm.

Daddy had Mommy pinned to the wall of their bedroom with one hand around her throat.

Daddy, please don't hurt Mommy anymore. Riley was by his side tugging on his arm before she'd even realized her feet had moved. A dangerous place to be.

He'd proven that in the next moment with the blow that had sent her sliding across the hard wood floor into the corner of the cherry-wood footboard.

With a blink, she returned to the table and settled onto one side of the cushioned bench.

Jalen watched her with that soft scrutiny of his that seemed to be able to cut past all the scar tissue to her very heart.

She wondered how long her thoughts had wandered. "No, I'm not doing this one for myself. I'm flipping it." She didn't add that every penny of profit she made on the places she remodeled and flipped went straight to women's shelters. So far, since Nate's death, she'd remodeled and flipped four houses and had donated the proceeds to a different shelter each time.

Jalen sat on the opposite cushion and kept his distance, for which she was thankful because this was suddenly seeming much too...something. Intimate? Desirable? Scary? Yes to all three. Especially when he was looking at her with such gentleness in his expression.

Terror clawed at her throat. "Do you mind saying grace?"

"Not at all." He bowed his head and offered up a quick prayer of thanks for the food, adding thanks that Rem had called to ease Riley's mind about where he was, and ending with a request for his continued safety.

And then the silence settled again as they dished food from the cardboard containers onto their plates.

She chastised herself. She'd known a lot of men from church between the Dad-and-Nate-years and now. Good men. Honest and loving men. She should be able to let the past go. Not all men were monsters.

Jalen took a slow bite of sweet and sour pork, studying her over the top of his wooden chopsticks. He chewed methodically while his gaze lingered leisurely. Searching... Analyzing... Admiring.

This was one of those good men. Her face heated and she suddenly took great interest in her chow mien noodles. She stirred them with her chopsticks but couldn't resist a peek back up at him. It had been two years. Could she let someone past the barriers she'd built up? *Should* she?

He grinned unrepentantly and swiped at his mouth with a paper napkin. "So...we lost contact a while back. Tell me what you've been up to the last year and a half."

Riley took her time, working at getting the next bite of noodles just-so on her chopsticks. He hadn't sounded angry that she'd essentially cut him off. And there was genuine interest in his question. The touch of guilt was coupled with regret. Where would things have gone for them if she hadn't broken off contact? Finally, realizing he still waited in that patient way of his, she shrugged. "Not much. Working at the elementary school as a teacher's aide now."

He nodded. "Knew that."

She paused. "You did?"

The soda can crinkled beneath his grip as he sipped slowly, watching her over the rim, then nodded as he set it back down. "I did."

She waved a hand around the interior of the room. "Been flipping some houses."

He twisted the can in a circle on the table. "Knew that too."

She pressed on, not wanting to contemplate the ramifications of his words at the moment. "Other than that I've just been helping Mom and Rem get by, and doing a little volunteer work at church."

"Heard you started a Sunday school class for survivors of abuse?" His angled gaze held concern. "How are you doing with that yourself?"

She'd nearly forgotten how direct he could be.

She wasn't sure how she felt about the fact that he'd obviously been checking up on her a little over the years. Thrilled and terrified all at once about covered it. What she did know was that she wasn't ready to talk with him about Dad. Or Nate. She ignored his last question and asked one of her own. "How do you know so much about what I've been doing?"

He shrugged. "Dakota must have mentioned it." A sly smile lifted one side of his lips. "I may have asked about you a time or two—or two hundred."

For a moment, Riley allowed the thrill to override the terror. She tilted her head. "Talking about me behind my back? I'm hurt." That flirtation was outrageous and she ought to be ashamed of herself.

Humor lingering in his eyes, he held up his phone and then set it next to her plate. "If you're willing to give me your number again, I can get my information straight from the source." The wink he tossed her was so quick she might have missed it if she'd blinked.

Her fingers trembled as she wiped them on a napkin. Her heart was beating so hard one might have thought the phone could leap up and slap her at any second. She should slide the device back to him, walk him to the door, and say goodnight. Or at the very least enter her number and then send him on his way. But the thought of painting alone tonight suddenly held very little appeal. "Hmm...my phone number is going to cost you."

"Oh yeah?" He chuckled and eased against the back of his bench, stretching his legs out so far that one of his feet touched her ankle. He folded his arms and raised his brows. "What'll it cost me?"

"Man power."

"Deal." He reached out and nudged the phone closer to her.

She laughed. "You don't even know what I need you to do yet."

With a quick shift of movement, he settled his arms on the table and leaned forward. "What I do know is that for the past year and a half I've thought about you every day. Wondered how you were. Wished we hadn't lost contact." He tilted his head. "I knew you needed some space...but now I'm hoping we can reconnect. So whatever you want me to do will be worth it." Another wink levered her pulse up one more notch.

She pretended to be thinking hard before she slowly lifted the phone and tapped in her number. A peek over the top of the screen revealed he was grinning from ear to ear. Face heating, she held it out to him.

He took it, studied the entry she'd just made, and then pressed the call button. From her purse, her phone rang. She didn't rise to get it, but cocked him a curious look.

He grinned and held up one finger, apparently listening to her voice mail greeting. After a moment he said, "Hi Riley. This is Jalen. Just wanted to make sure you had my number in your phone. Now you have no excuse not to call me the next time you need something." His gaze held a gentle humor touched with a hint of seriousness as he studied her across the table.

Her heart seemed to melt in her chest. She took a breath, held it, then eased it out slowly.

Jalen hung up the phone and then grinned at her outright. "Well I think my job here is done." With that, he stood and reached for the sports bag he'd chucked into the corner when they arrived. "Thanks. Have a good night." He took a deliberate step toward the door.

She laughed. "Don't even think about it, mister. Just head on down the hall and get ready to do some painting."

"Mind if I shower first?" He arched a brow.

She swallowed, not sure she wanted to contemplate him in the shower, with her just down the hall. She delayed a response by teasing, "So you're one of those guys who'll do anything to get out of a few minutes of work, huh?"

He chuckled. "Trust me you'll be a lot happier in cramped quarters with me if you let me rinse off the soccer practice."

"I don't keep towels or soap here."

He lifted his gym bag. "I have both."

"Sure then." She pointed through the living room. "The bathroom's the first door on the right down the hall."

"Thanks, I'll only be a few minutes."

"Sure that's what they all say," she called to his

retreating back.

His laughter drifted from the hall. She glanced around the room and realized how good it had felt to just converse, and enjoy a man's company. And yet...she pressed her lips together and one palm drifted to her lower abdomen...there were so many reasons she shouldn't let this go another step further. *Lord, do you see me down here? I'm trying to move on and put the past behind me, but there are some mistakes I'll never be able to escape. It wouldn't be fair for me to ask others to live with them too, now would it?* With a sigh, she rose and made quick work of cleaning up the kitchen.

She'd only been in the bedroom painting for a few minutes when, true to his word, he slipped through the door. She was standing on the old paint splattered chair she always used to reach the high corners. He stopped beside her, and his intoxicating cologne and shampoo combination wafted up to her. A longing to close her eyes and inhale more deeply nearly caught her off guard, but she stopped herself just in time.

She forced herself to be all business. "I'm on the final coat, so I'll do the cutting in near the ceiling if you don't mind manning the roller behind me? I'm going to put trim up around the floor, so just use that old piece of cardboard and get as close to the floor as possible but it doesn't have to be perfect because it will be covered by the trim."

He maintained his position and settled his hands on his hips. "Are you going to drip on me?

Because I happen to love this shirt."

She glanced down to see he was wearing an old green Seattle Sounders T-shirt that already had a hole in one shoulder. Glancing from him to the paint in her cup and back, she lifted her brush to draw his attention to the cerulean color. "Sounder colors are blue and green, so if this gets on your shirt it will just look like it's supposed to be there."

He growled good naturedly. "Woman, this is the lucky shirt that I wore for every game they won last season."

She angled him a look. "Which shirt did you wear for the games they lost?"

He brushed aside her question and bent to pick up the roller and work it into the paint in the tray. "Let's just say this shirt wielded more power on some days than others."

She laughed out loud. "My, that is a powerful shirt. I could get you a garbage bag to protect its mighty magic?"

He chuckled and ended the silliness with his lifted roller. "Alright, where do I start? Here good?" He pointed to the section just to her left.

She nodded and they settled into a quiet routine. Again the silence was companionable and comforting instead of awkward. Riley's iPad streamed Third Day from under the rag she'd tossed over it to protect it, and every once in awhile Jalen softly sang a few bars of a song.

She liked that more than she ought to. She didn't recall ever hearing Nate sing, much less to a

Christian song. They were nearly around the perimeter of the room now and Jalen had long since caught up to her and was working his roller over the section of wall in front of her now.

He bent down to run the roller along the floor line and—to avoid having to ask him to move—she leaned out a little farther than she normally would have. He stood at that exact moment and Riley's squeak of warning came too late.

Jalen's head connected with her cup of paint and the brush she was just dipping back into it. Both flew out of her hands.

The chair, which had already been precariously balanced due to her overextension, gave way to gravity and tipped out from under her.

Jalen saw the collision coming and tried to protect himself, but still had the paint roller in his hand when he curled his arms over his head.

Riley's stomach careened along the paint-filled sponge of the roller like luggage at an airport security check, before connecting with Jalen's elbow.

Only a nanosecond later the cup of trim paint bounced off Jalen's head and did a remarkable impression of a sprinkler as it sprayed an arc of cerulean blue across both of them.

With one swift sweep of his arms, Jalen had her tucked close in a protective gesture. He stumbled a few steps but managed to keep them on their feet. "Are you okay?"

Riley couldn't seem to pull in any air. Her

fingers fisted into the front of his shirt and her mouth opened and closed, but still no relief of oxygen filled her starved lungs.

And then after a moment of sheer panic, sweet air flowed in. Her whole body trembled and she gulped for another lungful.

Jalen dropped the paint roller he still clutched into the paint tray and then took her by the shoulders. "Riley are you okay?" True concern filled his tone.

She nodded. And eased out a long slow exhale. "Just had the wind knocked out of me for a second."

His hands stroked slowly up and down her upper arms. "Sorry." His concern melted the dark chocolate of his eyes to a creamy mocha. "Are you breathing okay now?"

She wasn't, but it had a lot more to do with the fact that he kept caressing her than with their collision, so she just nodded.

His hands kept stroking and she wished he would stop at the same time as she wanted to just close her eyes and revel in the feel of him so near.

His gaze lifted to her hair and his lips twitched.

She could feel the sticky wetness of the paint that must be drizzling down the side of her head. And he didn't look much better. One drip of paint trickled down his temple.

To avoid the inclination to reach up and swipe it away, she lowered her focus to where her fists had clenched handfuls of his shirt, leaving large blue splotches. She winced and reflexively swiped at the paint, but when her mind registered the firmness of the muscles below the material, she quickly snatched her hands behind herself.

She tucked her bottom lip between her teeth. "I think your lucky shirt just lost all its powers."

Humor crinkled the corners of his eyes but he didn't remove his attention from her face, or seem too concerned about his shirt.

His next words were low, and spoken in an almost serious tone. "You've gone and done it now, Riley Ross." Another caress of his palms against her arms sent a shiver up her back, and a wave of desire straight through her heart.

She should step away. But even though her brain sent feeble instructions to her legs, they seemed powerless to do her bidding.

His focus drifted from her eyes to roam her features and one of his hands slipped behind her and settled at the small of her back. Gently, he tugged her against him. "Riley." Her name was barely a whisper between them. His gaze dipped to her lips.

She settled her palms against his chest once more. "Jalen." She meant to hold him back and tell him this could go no further, but there was no rigidity in her arms and the words dammed up in her throat till she couldn't seem to dislodge them. To her chagrin, she wanted nothing more than to feel his lips on hers.

There was a request for permission in his eyes and the tilt of his chin.

She nodded ever so slightly and lifted up onto her toes, meeting him partway in a clash of lips that was at once hunger and restraint. Desire and self-control. Abandon and moderation. It was bliss and torture. Freedom yet captivity. The promise of a beautiful future, but tainted with the ugly reminder of what could never be. She groaned audibly and dropped back to her heels, effectively parting the kiss.

She gulped for air. "Jalen, I'm sorry. I can't—"

His own breaths fanned her forehead. "It's okay, I went too fast. When I came back to town, I meant to take this slower." He caressed his palm over the back of her head and pressed a kiss to her forehead.

His words tumbled around in her brain.

When I came back to town, I meant to take this slower.

She pondered the phrase. He'd planned for a relationship? Wanted her? Had he come back to town for other reasons than to be the soccer coach?

The realization awed her. But swift on the heels of that feeling came despair, sorrow, and futility. Her forehead still resting against his lips, she closed her eyes and willed away the tears. Forced herself to say the words. "Jalen, this can't go anywhere."

He leaned back and touched her chin, a quizzical lift to his brow. "Why not?"

How did she explain to him that it wasn't just him? But on the other hand it was especially him? That two years ago a fist had not only torn away the last tattered threads of her ability to trust another human being with her heart, but had also torn away any chance she would ever have of carrying another child. She wouldn't ask any man to walk through that with her, so she'd made a decision simply not to start any relationships. But she especially wouldn't ask it of a man who already made her wish so deeply that her grim reality could be altered.

And if she told him? He would only brush away her concerns as if they didn't matter. But they did matter, and that was what terrified her the most. If it wasn't a big deal now, someday it would be, and he would come to resent her.

Like she resented herself.

Riley, I said 'commere'!

Nate, please. Everything inside her quaked. Even the baby within her squirmed as though urging her to run. But it would only be worse for her once he caught her. And he would catch her, eventually.

Don't make me tell you 'gain!

His breath was foul. His hands clumsy with alcohol when they gripped her much too hard.

Where'd ya think you's gonna go, huh? Look at you... He pinched her face in one meaty hand until her lips protruded and her molars cut painfully into the soft skin of her cheeks. *You think anyone else would put up with a face as ugly as this?* The slap jolted her head back.

She tilted her face away. What had she ever seen

in him? Silence was her best ally.

Look at me. He shook her firmly with each of his next words, snapping her head so that it would have been impossible to follow his command. *Look. At. Me!*

Nate, please. She curled her hands around her head and bent to protect the small mound of her belly. *You're hurting me. Hurting the baby.*

Hurting you?

The laugh. She would never forget his laugh.

You haven't seen anything yet, Riley girl. Not a thing.

"Riley?" Jalen's concerned question jolted her back to the present. Hands cupped her face, stroked it gently. Hands that belonged to a man who would never dream of causing her pain. A man who made her long to give in and let go of the fight.

But she forced herself to consider what was fair and right. She would live with her penance. But she would never ask another to.

He was still waiting for an answer in that quiet way of his, dark eyes solemn.

She forced herself to step away from his touch, and glanced around at the room. Thankfully, she'd had the carpet fully covered with plastic because paint was splattered all over the floor. She lifted the roller and cleaned up the few trickles on the wall.

He followed her. Touched her hand. Took the

roller from her and returned it to the tray. "Talk to me, Riley. Why can't this go anywhere?"

"It's complicated, Jalen. It just can't—" Her phone chimed from her back pocket. She swiped her hands against her jeans and snagged it free. Her eyes closed in relief as she recognized the same number Rem had called from before. And she was honest enough to admit that a little of her relief was because this would save her from further time with Jalen.

She tapped to answer. "Rem?"

"Hey. We're pulling into town now."

Thank you, Jesus! "I'll meet you at Thrift and Save." Shoving the phone back in her pocket she said, "We have to go. Rem will be there in just a couple minutes."

Jalen wiped his hands on a rag and motioned to the still unpainted section of the wall. "Let me stay and finish up for you?"

Yes. That would be good. The more distance she put between herself and this man right now, the better. "Yeah. Sure. In fact, if you don't mind...just make sure the door is locked on your way out, would you?"

He dipped his chin and drilled her with a look that said he knew she was running from him.

She didn't care if he knew it, because he was right. She held up her key ring. "I have my keys. And I should probably get Rem right home. He's had a long day." She started down the hall, calling over her shoulder, "Thanks for your help tonight."

She halfway wished he would call out to stop her, but silence was the only thing that followed her out to her car.

Disappointment mingled with relief.

But even at that, she somehow knew Jalen Rivera didn't consider the conversation over.

Chapter 4

Sunday morning, Dakota Trask reveled in the feel of Justus's fingers laced between hers. They made their way through the foyer of the church greeting people as they went. Texts, emails, and phone calls just couldn't compare to actually having the man here by her side. The last time they'd spent more than a few hours together on a weekend had been last Christmas. And now he was here to stay. Looking for work nearby. Her feeling of contentment couldn't get much higher. It was so wonderful to have him close.

He'd hardly let go of her hand since he'd scooted onto the bench beside her and leaned close to settle a kiss against her temple this morning.

They finally escaped the press of people and stepped into the parking lot. Warm September sunshine streamed down, heating the air to just-perfect. A bee droned by. And high above them one gull called to another.

When they reached her car there was a long-stemmed red rose, wrapped in tissue and plastic, tucked beneath her windshield wipers.

"Entertaining other admirers, Dakota? For shame!" Justus's voice was serious but the twinkle in his blue eyes gave him away.

Dakota chuckled. "What did you do?" She reached for the rose and found a note attached. Folding it open, she took a moment to read. There was no signature but the words were penned in Justus's distinctive scrawl.

She lifted him a look. "Well apparently this secret admirer wants to take me to lunch at Fisherman's Wharf. And since I'm starving, I think I'll have to take him up on his offer, so you have a good afternoon." She offered him a cheeky grin.

He chuckled and stepped into her personal space, settling his hands at her waist. "So you're just going to go off with this unknown guy and leave me in the lurch?"

She raised the velvet petals to her nose and lingered over the scent, then scrunched up her face into a thoughtful look and nodded. Lifting the flower, she tilted her head. "He did give me a rose, so he can't be too dangerous."

"Hmmm..." He bent and brushed a wisp of a kiss across her forehead. "Do you know how good it is to be able to touch you while we are talking?"

She stretched up on her tiptoes and wrapped her arms around his neck. "Funny, I was just thinking the same thing a little earlier. Skype is nice when it's necessary, but this is nicer." Her lips grazed his for just a moment before she settled back to her normal height and turned her attention back to the rose. She tapped him on the chest with it. "Unfortunately for you, this other guy gave me a rose, so I have to run. Seems like he might be a close contender for my attentions."

He pressed his forehead to hers and looked deeply into her eyes. "Close contender, huh? I've apparently not been doing my job well enough if one little rose from this other guy is turning your head."

Dakota pretended to think. "That's right. The last time you sent me flowers was on my birthday. Hmmm, yes, I really think I should go find out who this other admirer is."

Justus sighed dramatically. "Fine. But don't expect our relationship to ever be the same if you go through with this."

Her heart rate kicked up a bit at that. She knew the rose was from him and they were both just being silly. But had he meant more by that last comment? Her mouth went dry. There was a certain intensity to his expression that she never remembered seeing before.

He pulled away before she could analyze it further. "Run along then. You don't want to be late." He winked conspiratorially and jauntily walked toward his Z3 a few spaces down.

Dakota chuckled and slipped into her seat behind the wheel. The fifteen minutes it would take to drive to the restaurant could not go by fast enough.

When she arrived and gave the maître d' her name, he immediately gestured for her to follow him. "We have a table reserved for you right this way, ma'am."

He ushered her to an intimate table for two tucked into a curtained alcove on the restaurant's ocean-facing deck. Across her plate lay a small bouquet of two roses interspersed with baby's breath. The card on this bouquet simply read, *You take my breath away.*

She sank into her seat and blinked back tears of happiness. She was just turning to look out over the water when Justus's approach caught her eye.

He had changed into a black tux with a royal navy vest and bowtie that brought out the stunning blue of his eyes. Despite the soft breeze wafting all around her, oxygen suddenly seemed scarce. He offered a lopsided grin as he approached, but when he took in her face, concern replaced the smile.

He squatted down in front of her instead of taking his seat, a small frown furrowing his brow. "What's the matter?"

She shook her head. "These are happy tears."

Relief eased the lines of worry somewhat. "I see..." Still a question lingered in the tautness of his features. "Are you sure?"

She smiled through her blurred vision and leaned down to touch her forehead to his. "Oh, trust me, I'm sure. What did you do to my poor secret admirer?"

His grin was back. "I knocked him out cold in the parking lot."

A laugh bubbled free and her happiness threatened to spill over into another round of tears. "Poor guy."

Justus's hand came up to cup her cheek. "I think he'll survive. Are you sure you're okay?"

She nodded again and laid a kiss against his palm. "You just make me so happy."

His thumb stroked a warm path over her cheekbone. "I'm kinda glad to hear that. I was a little worried when you agreed to run off to eat with this other guy so easily."

She chuckled and poked him in the chest. "You goofball." She attempted to change the subject. "You changed into a tux..."

"Mmmhmm..." But other than that small acknowledgement, he didn't elaborate. "Should we eat?"

She nodded. But she didn't want to eat. She wanted him to get to asking her the question she knew he was here to ask her. Because she couldn't wait to throw her arms around him and tell him, yes, yes, yes!

He tortured her through a round of hors d'oeuvres that was delivered with a bouquet of three roses. And a course of soup that arrived with a bouquet of four. She ate methodically, every nerve in her body singing with anticipation and excitement.

He skillfully evaded all her questions about what

he was up to, but she could tell by the humor glinting in his eyes that he knew she knew. And that only added to the expectation buzzing through her like so much caffeine on an empty stomach.

Dinner was served with five roses tucked into a cocoon of ferns. And the dessert of chocolate mousse drizzled with raspberry sauce came accompanied by six more deep red blooms. "Justus, it's too much," she whispered, even as she admired and inhaled the aroma of the new flowers.

"Never." His eyes sparkling, he dipped his spoon into the mousse and held the bite out to her.

The smooth chocolate and tart raspberries were the perfect combination. She closed her eyes and savored the moment. The soft song of the surf, the cry of a gull high overhead, the whisper of the breeze through the curtains, the gentle strains of a violin... A violin? Her eyes popped open.

Next to their table, just outside the soft gossamer curtains, a violinist played the lilting melody. Justus no longer sat across from her. He was on one knee at her side, a look of sheer love shining in his eyes.

She covered her mouth with a trembling hand. "Justus..." the word was barely audible.

"Dakota..." Her name emerged a bit garbled. He swallowed, cleared his throat and started again as he reached into his jacket pocket. "Dakota, the last couple years with you have been some of the best years of my life. I love you more than I ever dreamed was even possible before we met."

She tilted her head and willed the tears to remain at bay. Her heart, so full of emotion at the moment, choked off any hope she might have had of responding with words.

Justus's brow furrowed. "But they've been torture too…"

She blinked. She hadn't been expecting that. What—

—And then he smiled and pulled a velvet box out to where she could see it. "I think we've spent enough time apart. And I hope you do too, because" —he opened the lid to reveal a diamond solitaire cocooned in swirls of gold and shimmering rubies— "I want you to be my wife. Will you marry me?"

"Oh, Justus!" She was down on her knees with him in a heartbeat, her arms flung around his neck. "Yes, yes, yes. A thousand times yes." She pulled back just far enough to cup his face in her palms. "You make me so happy. I love you."

A low sound of pleasure escaped his throat and his lips settled on hers.

She'd been wrong earlier.

Her feeling of contentment had just rocketed past anything she'd been feeling earlier and soared into the stratosphere.

Monday morning Riley stepped into the courtroom, her heart in her throat. She'd been prepared for the worst when it came to Mom's hearing, but she'd just learned from Mom's attorney that Mom was going to waive her right to a trial and plead guilty. So what had been slated to be her arraignment was now going to be a sentencing hearing.

On top of that, early this morning she'd finally received a call from Dad. The gist of that conversation was that Dad didn't want the hassle of raising his son and, according to him, Rem was old enough to fend for himself if Mom ended up serving extended time. *A freshman!* Riley had wanted to cuss Dad from here to Indiana and back, but had somehow managed to hold her tongue.

She hadn't been able to hold back her tears though, once she'd hung up. She'd cried not for herself but for Rem. A kid deserved two parents that loved and cared for him. Rem had certainly gotten a raw deal in the parental love and nurture department. The only thing she could do was give him as much love as she could possibly muster. She could raise him. And that's exactly what she intended to tell the judge. She and Rem would weather this storm together and hopefully be stronger people for it, in the end.

But, as if her battle wasn't already difficult enough, she'd also learned that because of the surety of Mom serving time, Rem's temporary custody would be on the docket this morning. Judge Alicia Mason ran her courtroom with a conservative iron fist and had apparently declared there was no point in delaying a decision about

Rem once she'd made a decision about Mom.

And her father's brother was contesting Riley's request for custody of Rem.

She clenched her teeth together. She hadn't seen Uncle Doyle since she was in elementary school. And as far as she knew, Rem had only met the man once. Doyle only wanted Rem for the checks he would get from Dad for his care.

Remington and Riley's attorney had been called in. Riley had just left him and Rem to discuss final details, but the game plan was to get her brother remanded over to Riley's custody.

Riley settled into a chair in the front row of the public seating area of the courtroom and glanced at the clock on the wall. Ten minutes. Someone sank into the seat beside her and she looked over.

Jalen.

Her heart skittered to a halt, and then kicked into overtime.

Wearing a brown suit and a deep red tie, he looked better than any man had a right to.

His soft mocha gaze skimmed over her before returning to her own.

So many questions and promises lingered in his eyes. *How are you holding up? Is it okay if I sit here? This will all be over soon. You are going to make it. Hang in there.*

She'd never known anyone who could say so much without saying a word.

The scent of his cologne, sporty and fresh, wafted to her, slamming home the memory of their kiss. She felt telltale warmth in her cheeks and forced her focus into her lap. She hadn't seen him all day Saturday. And she'd somehow managed to avoid him at church yesterday, but even a couple days apart hadn't faded the memory of the wonderful sensations elicited by his lips on hers. In fact, if anything, it might have heightened it.

They'd never finished the conversation about how they could never be together. Pain sliced through her just at the thought. Why did doing the right thing have to be so hard? Things would sure be easier right now if she'd just resisted the temptation to kiss him in the first place!

"Morning," he finally said.

She nodded a greeting. "Morning." She pressed her lips together, unable to decide if having him nearby eased some of her anxiety or increased it.

Movement drew her attention to the back of the room. A couple reporters and their cameramen were setting up in the space behind the back row. She bit her lip. Of course there would be reporters here. She should have expected it. After all, Mom had driven her car at full speed into the front wall of the town's only grocery store. And they would also be curious about the fate of the local millionaire's son.

Riley swung back to face the front.

Jalen leaned closer. "I'm praying for you."

"Thanks." His words reminded her that she should probably be doing some praying of her own.

Lord, please just be in the details today. Be with

Mom. Help her to heal up both physically and mentally. Help her to find her worth in a relationship with You. Please help me to get custody of Rem. I've heard this judge can be a little hardnosed. Just help her to be merciful and understanding today, please. For Rem's sake. He needs me right now.

A door at the front of the court room opened up and Mom shuffled in, escorted by a female officer who resembled a grizzly bear in tennis shoes. Mom's orange jumpsuit only highlighted the purple bruising around both eyes and across her swollen and split-skinned nose. Her face must have smashed into the steering wheel. The back of one of her hands was nearly black. That bruise disappeared under the plaster of the cast on her arm and looked even more painful than the ones on her face. Mom's expression remained lifeless even when she noticed Riley sitting just behind the bar near her defendant's table. Without even an acknowledging nod, she dropped into the chair the officer pulled out for her as though she'd just lost all the strength from her legs. Her indifference hurt like a slap to the face.

A warm touch drew her attention down to see Jalen's broad brown fingers covering both her hands that she had fisted in her lap. Her fingernails were biting into her palms. She eased in a slow inhale and forced herself to relax.

Seemingly relieved that he'd helped ease her tension a little, Jalen squeezed her hands softly and started to pull away.

But, as if on reflex, she clutched hold of him, and then realized what she'd done. What had she just been telling herself about resisting temptation? Discouragement rolling through her, she quickly let go.

Why did this have to be so difficult? Couldn't she just let her guard down for a little bit and have a normal relationship with this wonderful man?

His hand stayed where it was, hovering over hers for a moment, and then his fingers slipped across her palm to slowly intertwine with her own. All the while she could feel the intensity of his scrutiny on her face.

Just for now. Riley gave in to her weakness and didn't withdraw from him again.

It was silly, not to mention emotionally dangerous, to feel the need to have him there holding her. Especially since she'd already told him this could go nowhere. It would only make the conclusion of the conversation she needed to have with him harder, but with all that she was facing at the moment she couldn't seem to find the willpower to do the right thing and let him go. She glanced over and mouthed, "Thank you."

He nodded.

"All rise!"

Jalen stood beside her, strong and steady, like a life preserver in the midst of a stormy sea.

Rem and his attorney slipped onto the bench on the other side of Riley.

Judge Mason was shorter than Riley had

pictured her, and much more petite. Her graying hair curled around her sun-spotted face and rectangular spectacles. She lowered herself into her seat at the bench and eyed the courtroom above her glasses. "Thank you. You may all be seated."

Mom's hearing was short. Her attorney placed a guilty plea on her behalf and the prosecutor mentioned he had video footage from the surveillance equipment at Thrift and Save if the judge wanted to see it.

The judge waved a hand to dismiss the idea. "We don't need to take the time for that since she's pleading guilty, counselor."

Rem squirmed beside her and Riley felt her own relief that they'd been spared the sight of Mom's Jag crashing into the brick façade. Jalen's thumb stroked a warm trail along the side of her hand and she was thankful once again for his steady presence.

Judge Mason asked for concluding statements, both of which were short, and then she pronounced that because Mom had been driving under the influence, and for the third time since her license had been revoked, she was sentencing her to eighteen months with mandatory blood screenings, and rehab meetings.

All the strength seemed to ebb from Riley's body. She'd expected several months. Maybe a year at most.

Even with credit for time served, it would be well into the next school year before Mom got out.

Mom was escorted from the room and left

without even a backward glance at her two children sitting on the front row.

"Now, let's see..." Judge Mason studied the docket in front of her. She called out Rem's case and took a sip of water as she waited for the respective attorneys and clients to take their positions. Remington's lawyer presented a few facts and then stated that Riley would like to be given temporary custody of Remington until his mother could once again resume her role in his life.

Judge Mason peered at the attorney over her spectacles. "And is this sister here in the court?"

"She is, Your Honor." He swept a hand in Riley's direction.

And, as previously instructed, she stood to her feet, reluctantly leaving Jalen's comforting grip behind.

"Hmmm," the judge's gaze skimmed her from head to toe. "She's not much older than he is."

"She's ten years his senior, Your Honor."

"Very well, you may retake your seat, Miss Ross." The judge nodded at her, pinched lips offering neither approval nor disapproval. Her focus swung to the opposing attorney. "And what does your client have to say about this case?"

"Your Honor, my client is contesting Miss Ross's ability to care for her brother. He feels it is important to remind the court that Miss Ross formerly resided with a man who repeatedly endangered her. In fact at one point she was beaten so badly that she lost their child."

Jalen stiffened enough that she felt the bump of his shoulder against her own. He'd already known about Nate, and her abuse, so his anger had to be directed at her uncle for bringing it up.

Riley frowned. Of course Uncle Doyle would dredge up her relationship with Nate. She should have expected that. But she hadn't. *Please God, don't let my past mistakes prevent me from getting custody of Rem.*

The twist of the judge's lips was decidedly unfriendly this time. "Get to your point, counselor."

"My point being, Your Honor, that while Miss Ross remains unattached at this moment, she is still of a young impressionable age with a proven track record of associating herself with dangerous characters. The boy's uncle is concerned for his safety due to this reason, should he, too, be given into her custody."

Judge Mason leaned in to the back of her chair and tapped a pen on the bench. "Really, Counselor, if that's all your client has backing his—"

"There's more, Your Honor... If I could approach the bench?"

Riley's mouth was as dry as driftwood, and her heart was pounding so hard everyone in the courtroom could probably have heard it if silence had settled for a moment. She wasn't going to get custody. What was going to happen to Rem? Uncle Doyle lived hours away in Eugene. *Jesus, please...*

"Come, come." The judge waved impatiently for the man to approach as though she might have a round of golf she was late for and this trial was keeping her from it.

"I would like to submit these statements from several citizens regarding the fact that just last Friday while in the temporary care of his sister, Remington Ross skipped out on almost a full day of school and went all the way to Portland before his sister even knew he was missing."

Riley gasped. How had he found out about that? And would they really use something like that against her now?

At his table, Remington squirmed in his seat.

Judge Mason squinted at the paper presented to her and then peered at the attorney over her bifocals. "And you are prepared to call on these witnesses if it proves necessary?"

"I am, Your Honor. I also have these statements"—he pulled another sheet of paper from the folder in his hands—"stating that there have been several nights when she left the boy home alone."

That was a lie!

Judge Mason's horrified expression darted to Riley for the briefest of moments before a cloak of composure fell over her features and she focused on the new evidence before her. Sighing dramatically she tossed the papers onto the bench and leaned back in her seat, tapping steepled fingers to her lips. Her gaze drilled into the ceiling tiles at one corner of the room. Collectively those in attendance seemed to hold their breath.

Finally the judge threw up her hands. "Very well, bring in your witnesses, Counselor."

Riley thought her heart might just quit working right then and there.

Chapter 5

Riley listened to one witness after another recount the details of how Rem had skipped school and gone to Portland. How she hadn't known where he was, and how she'd been searching for him after soccer practice. The attorney even brought in the trucker who had picked up Rem while he was hitchhiking and given him a ride home from Portland.

After that, the man delved into her history, bringing in a couple of witnesses who had tried to talk her into leaving Nate multiple times.

Riley blinked as the next witness took the stand. Dakota!

Dakota looked pale and ill at ease. She glanced at Riley and there was so much pain in that one glance that Riley felt the bottom drop out of her stomach.

Dakota's testimony would certainly be damaging, but Riley couldn't feel anything but pity for her. There was no way Dakota would be up there unless they'd forced her to be.

"It's okay," Riley mouthed to her.

Dakota blinked and pinched her lips together in a grim look of defeat.

The attorney paced before the podium. "Miss Trask, please tell us how long you've known Miss Riley Ross."

"A couple years." Dakota brushed a strand of hair from her eyes.

"And in what capacity did you first come to know Miss Ross?"

"I was a counselor at House of Hope when Riley moved in."

"And House of Hope is a shelter for battered women, is it not?"

Dakota looked like she'd rather bite the man's head off than answer his question. "It is."

He pressed her for every detail until she was forced to reveal Riley's complete physical condition at the time she had moved to House of Hope.

Riley shuddered at the memory of how lost and helpless she'd felt at that time. And then she'd met Jalen not long after. She glanced over at him.

His jaw was working back and forth like a mad bull about to charge.

And suddenly a sense of peace filled her. That sludge at the bottom of the barrel was exactly where God had needed to take her in order to reach her. It wasn't until then that she'd recognized her need.

It would be the same this time. She wasn't going

back on the lessons she'd learned now. Whether she got custody of Rem or not, she had to trust that God was working in all this. Bringing about the good He desired. Because she definitely loved Him.

She squeezed Jalen's hand.

He glanced over. His face was hard, but he squeezed her hand back.

And that was enough.

When she looked back up, Dakota was leaving the stand, and then came the doctor who had delivered her stillborn child the night Nate had beaten her so badly just before he killed himself.

This lawyer was obviously slated to get a nice percentage of each of Uncle Doyle's custody checks if they won because he was certainly pulling out all the stops.

Beside her Jalen was stiff, every muscle and breath taut with anger.

Riley couldn't quite tell if he was angry with her for the way she'd endangered her child, or with the attorney who was dredging all this up. But when she tried to pull her hand from his, he tightened his grip and kept her there, which made her feel better.

The judge on the other hand—her face grew more distraught with every word that was spoken.

Finally, the attorney said he had no more witnesses. The judge asked if Riley's attorney had any rebuttal and he said, "Your honor, I'd like to call Miss Riley Ross to the stand."

Riley's legs almost didn't have the strength to carry her to the box and keep her upright as she was sworn in. He asked her some preliminary questions like how she was related to Remington, and where she lived. Then he asked her the question they'd rehearsed. "Miss Ross, why do you want custody of your brother?"

They'd practiced a long-winded answer with all the political aspects the judge would be expecting to hear, but when her gaze landed on Remington looking so forlorn at his table, only one answer would come to mind. "Because I love him and he needs me. We need each other."

Her attorney gave her a subtle nod, as if that was a brilliant answer and then pressed on with their planned questions. "Miss Ross, you've heard a lot of damaging testimony about yourself today. Would you care to defend yourself?"

This question she answered as they'd practiced. "No. Except for one accusation. Everything stated here today has been true. I used to live with an abusive man, and many people tried to talk me into leaving him. But I'm different now. I gave my life to Jesus two years ago and with His love, I'm not the same person I used to be. I completed the full treatment course at House of Hope and graduated a year ago. I've remained committed to what they taught me and attend church regularly. The only thing I would contradict is that I haven't left Remington home alone all night like they made it sound. I have left him up at our house in the Bluffs and then returned to town on a couple nights to finish some work on a house I'm remodeling. But

I've been home by eleven each night and our housekeeper lives in an apartment above the garage, so if anything had happened he could have gone to her for help."

Her attorney steepled his fingers. "And did Remington run off to Portland last week?"

She swallowed. "He did. But then he felt bad and came home."

"And who did he call when he was on his way home?"

"He called me."

He gave her a nod of assurance. "That will be all, Miss Ross. Thank you for your time."

"Cross examine?" The judge asked the other attorney.

He declined.

"Any other witnesses, counselor?" the judge asked as Riley returned to her seat.

Riley's attorney called Remington to the stand.

Riley felt sure that if she had eaten any breakfast that morning, she would at this very moment be in the ladies' room casting it up. She would have given just about anything to spare Remington from going through this.

Remington looked small in the witness box, his head and shoulders barely rising above the low wall that separated it from the rest of the room. But when his attorney asked him how old he was, his voice rang out clear and firm. "Fourteen."

"And do you have a preference of whom you'd rather live with while your mom is incarcerated?"

Remington nodded. "I do."

Riley held her breath. Please, Rem, don't do anything stupid.

"And who would that be?" Remington's attorney paced before the stand.

"My sister, Riley."

Riley's relief rushed out in an audible release of air.

Jalen hadn't taken her hand again, but he reached over now and patted her knee with a smile of support.

"Why do you want to live with your sister?"

"Because, for as long as I can remember, she's been the one who's taken care of me. And because I've only ever met my uncle once, and he only wants me so he can have the money from the support checks my dad will send him."

"Objection!" Uncle Doyle's attorney jumped to his feet. "The boy can't know the reasons. My client has his best interests at heart, Your Honor."

The judged waved him back into his seat. "Sit down, counselor. Objection granted."

Remington's lawyer said he had no more questions, and Uncle Doyle's lawyer declined a cross examination, apparently afraid of what Rem might say to any of his questions. So their attorney gave a few words in closing.

Everything he'd offered up seemed paltry and inadequate in the face of all the recriminations the court had heard about her this morning, but it was going to have to do. She didn't have anything but the truth on her side.

Riley realized the time for the judge to offer her decision had arrived as silence settled.

The judge simply stared at the podium in front of her for a long minute. Then she glanced up as though suddenly realizing there were people waiting for her to make a decision.

Her gaze bounced off Riley's as she banged her gavel. "Court will recess for thirty minutes while I consider my judgment on this case."

Everyone stumbled to their feet as the judge rose and made a hasty exit.

Riley realized she was chewing on her fingernail and yanked her hands down, folding them in front of her. Her stomach still felt like it might empty its contents right there in front of everyone.

Rem turned from where he was standing and gave her a pleading look that held an apology and a cry for help all in one. Uncle Doyle turned and glowered at her, causing her stomach to drop. She frowned. Shouldn't they all be on the same side here? Wanting only what was best for Rem?

Jalen cupped one hand to the back of her neck and squeezed gently, and she had to admit she didn't know what she would have done without him there by her side. "Jalen, thanks for being with me. Win or lose, God's in control. I'm trying to remember that. But it helps to have...a friend."

His hand tightened. "I wouldn't be anywhere else."

Dakota approached, wearing an expression of

uncertainty. Taysia was by her side, looking like she was there for moral support, her one-year-old daughter, Zoe, on her hip.

Riley leapt out of her seat and threw her arms around Dakota. "It's okay."

"I'm so sorry! They forced me with a subpoena."

"Don't be sorry. You only told the truth."

Riley also gave Taysia a quick hug and pinched Zoe's chubby cheek, eliciting a cute grin around her pacifier.

Taysia offered a smile of encouragement. "Marie said to tell you she's praying. She's covering the gym for me today so she can't be here."

"I know she'd be here if she could." Riley turned back to Dakota.

There was moisture in Dakota's eyes. "What they didn't let me say was that you are not the same woman today that you were back then. You've figured out you are special and valuable. And I should have been allowed to say so."

"Thanks. At least *I* was allowed to say so. Hopefully the judge will keep that in mind." Riley squeezed Dakota's hand and that was when she felt the ring. Her eyes widened and she glanced down. The rock sparkling on Dakota's finger was surrounded by rubies, and graced her hand perfectly. "Dakota!"

Dakota's face pinked, and just then Justus stepped up by her side.

Jalen grinned and held out a hand to the man. "Congratulations, my friend. When's the big day?"

Justus shook his hand, but his gaze slid to Dakota. "We're still discussing that."

Dakota blinked innocently. "For some reason the man thinks three months is too long to be engaged."

Riley did her best to smile at the levity of the moment. "I'm sure you two will get it all figured out."

Jalen turned his attention to Zoe then, making faces and crazy noises. She giggled and held out her pacifier to him, as though she wanted to share it.

Riley smiled. Zoe was so adorable. She had Kylen's dark curls, and Taysia's blue gray eyes, soft round cheeks, and always a ready smile. Riley didn't think she'd ever heard the baby cry.

Jalen pretended to gobble up the pacifier, much to Zoe's delight. She giggled and tucked her head shyly into Taysia's shoulder. But after only a few seconds she must have changed her mind, because she turned back to him and held out her arms, leaning toward him, and obviously wanting him to hold her.

"Wow," Taysia said as she passed the baby over to him. "That's high praise, coming from this one. She's always more than willing to flirt, but only so long as it's from the safety of Kylen's or my arms."

Dakota poked Jalen's shoulder. "Jalen is like a baby magnet. Every time I've been at his and Justus's old church he's had a different baby in his arms."

Justus clapped Jalen on one shoulder. "You

better get busy finding a woman to give you a passel of your own kids."

Justus's words might not have carried so much punch except that right at that moment Jalen looked at Riley as he bent to blow a raspberry against one of Zoe's little cheeks. She felt the look all the way to her toes. The man obviously wanted children of his own one day. *Deserved* to have children of his own one day.

Dakota and Taysia, who both knew Riley's situation, exchanged glances.

Dakota cleared her throat and took Justus's hand. "How about we go get a coffee before the judge comes back in?" She cast Riley an apologetic look, her gaze bouncing to Jalen and back, before ending with a sad smile and a wink of encouragement as she and Justus walked away.

Riley swallowed away the remorse and depression that threatened to blanket her. No matter how nice it had felt to have Jalen's support today. No matter how much she wanted to give in and see if a relationship between them might work, she had to let that desire go and quit being selfish.

For his sake.

She needed to end this right away before it got any more complicated and difficult.

Chapter 6

Riley's heart felt like it was being ripped from her chest as she watched Jalen hand the baby back to Taysia.

Taysia said she was going to run change Zoe and headed towards the lobby, after another quick hug to Riley's neck.

Riley and Jalen resumed their seats. Riley fiddled with the ring on one finger for a minute trying to work up the courage to do what she knew needed to be done. If she didn't cut the strings right now she might never have the strength to do so.

She looked over at him. "Jalen, I really appreciate you being here. But you don't have to hang out here all morning. I'm sure you have other things to do. I'll be fine."

He only looked at her with that gently intense expression that almost made her feel like he could read her mind. For a long moment he didn't say anything. His gaze moved beyond her to the door that Taysia and Zoe had just exited through. And then he looked back at her, a slight furrow in his brow. "I wouldn't be anywhere else."

She pressed her lips together. Nodded. Tucked her thumbnail between her teeth. She dared not say any more. The man was far too perceptive for her good. Once today was over. Once he wasn't sitting by her side all supportive and enticing, then she'd find the strength to push him away.

The minutes dragged by after that, and if Jalen hadn't given her an old receipt from his back pocket with the instructions "Here, torture this," all her nails would have been gone by the time the judge came back into the room.

As it was, when the woman did reappear, the receipt was a little pile of shredded pills on the seat beside her.

Riley kept her hands firmly fisted and as far from Jalen as possible this time, determined to begin dealing on her own with whatever the situation would be.

Judge Mason peered at the courtroom over her bifocals.

Riley held her breath, afraid to miss even one word as the judge began her decision.

"First I'd like to say that I believe every young man who is Remington Ross's age ought to have a strong father figure in his life. It is the court's opinion that the lack of a good father-figure is what has filled so many of our jails with young men and women."

Riley's world turned black around the edges.

Uncle Doyle was going to win custody!

As if he sensed it too, her uncle turned and offered her a triumphant smile.

"Second, I would like to say that this has not been an easy decision for me." The judge paused and sipped from a glass of water.

Riley felt like she just might leap across the bar and shake the ruling from the woman. She gripped the edges of her seat to keep herself from doing anything rash.

The courtroom was so quiet that the judge's glass reconnecting with her podium was distinctly heard. "While Miss Ross can and should be held responsible for her past actions, it appears to the court as though she's turned over a new leaf and is doing her best to move on from some admittedly big red flags. What she can't be held responsible for are the actions of her brother who is obviously young and rash. The fact that it was to her he turned when he was returning home and not to anyone else speaks volumes to their relationship, and to Miss Ross's care for the boy." She paused for another sip of water.

Riley gripped her seat so hard that her arms ached. If the woman took one more drink she just might throttle her!

Judge Mason skimmed the room, her focus flitting first from Rem, then to Riley, and finally on to Uncle Doyle.

Jesus please...

"Thus it is my judgment that Remington Dylan

Ross be remanded over to the temporary custody of his sister." Judge Mason's gavel fell with a loud *smack*, and she gathered her papers and exited the courtroom.

Riley sat stock still for only a fraction of a second and then she was on her feet, through the bar, and with her arms around Remington's neck. *Thank you, Jesus. Thank you, Jesus. Thank you, Jesus.*

"Riley!" Remington pushed her away. "It's not like we didn't drive here together this morning. Just chill."

But Riley could tell from the spark of life in his eyes that he was just as happy about the decision as she was.

She mussed his hair. "And it's not like I'm not going to have chores for you to do when we get home today, either."

He groaned audibly.

Riley didn't care. She was just so relieved, she wanted to cry. One hurdle down and only another year or lifetime of them to go. She sighed.

Uncle Doyle grumbled something to his lawyer and then brushed by them without even pausing to say hello. And Riley couldn't say she was sorry to see his back as he slapped open the courtroom doors and stormed from the room.

At the rear of the room, Dakota and Taysia had their arms around each other, their heads tipped together, and big smiles on their faces as they looked at her. Baby Zoe bounced up and down gleefully on Taysia's hip, as though she too were rejoicing in the decision. The girls both gave her a thumbs-up.

Riley smiled her thanks for their support.

Her gaze connected with Jalen's. His hands in the pockets of his slacks, he was watching her with a tender expression of joy on his face.

Every young man ought to have a strong father-figure in his life. The judge's words came back to her and she felt an urgent sense of responsibility toward her brother.

Maybe she would ask Jalen if he would mind spending some extra time with Remington, but only for Remington. She would steel herself from anything more personal. In fact she would just stay as far away as possible when Jalen was around.

And she would work at reshoring up the walls around her heart, because the man seemed to be able to breach them without even trying.

Jalen stood by his rig and watched Riley hurry Remington to her Jeep. He jingled his keys in his pocket and clamped his tongue with his side teeth. Something had changed in there and he couldn't quite put his finger on what it was. One minute he was thinking maybe he hadn't blown things with her as badly as he'd feared the other night, and the next she was stiffer than a desiccated starfish.

She pulled from the parking lot not even giving

him a second glance.

Ouch.

Sighing, he pressed the unlock button on his key fob, pulled open his door, and slid into his seat. But for a long minute he rested his wrists against the top of the wheel and just stared out at the hedge on the other side of the walkway in front of his rig.

His sister Celina's face came to mind. When was the last time he'd thought of her? It had been so many years and he'd only been young when her husband had punched her, hurtling her across a room where she'd struck her head and died. But he remembered Mama's worry and fretting in the months before that. They'd all known something wasn't right. Celina, normally so confident and full of life, had become distant and guarded.

Guarded.

That was the perfect word to describe Riley. Jalen knew she'd been abused by Nate. And he suspected she'd been abused, especially emotionally, by her father too.

Lord... He lowered his forehead to the steering wheel. *Help me to give her what she needs. I know what I want, but help me to put her first. She's already had so many people misuse her. I don't want to be added to that list. So give me patience, Father. Where I would rush in and press for my way, remind me to give her space and time. But help her to see that You know the plans You have for her and that they are to prosper her and not to harm her. To give her a hope and a future.*

With a breath, he forced himself to start the rig. Back out of his slot. Pull onto the street.

His hands were tight around the steering wheel and he forced them to relax.

He would give her time. He wouldn't call her unless she opened the door to it first. But... *Lord...* That didn't mean he wouldn't be praying like a mad man in the meantime.

The next day Riley sat in the visitation area of the local jail and waited for an officer to bring Mom in. Mom would be transferred to a bigger facility, probably by the end of the week, but for now she was still being held in the Marinville jail, and Riley had wanted to visit her right away because after she got transferred she would be several hours away and it would be more difficult to find the time to go see her.

She'd been praying all morning about what she was going to say to her, and she still wasn't sure she had all the right words.

Riley couldn't help but wince when Mom stepped into the visitation room.

If anything, her bruising looked worse today than it had yesterday. Her hair was in a wild disarray and her hands trembled visibly when she sank onto the plastic chair on the other side of the table. Her cast *thunked* against the table when she settled her hands there.

Riley reached over and took her fingers between her own. Once Mom got into a bigger facility, they might be separated by Plexiglas for visitations. Would this be the last time she got to touch her mother for over a year?

There were so many questions she wanted to ask. So many reassurances she wanted to offer. But she had no idea where to start, so she simply bracketed Mom's hands and tried not to blubber like a baby.

Mom hung her head and played with her fingernails. "I guess I was pretty stupid. I don't even remember leaving Pete's that night."

Riley held her silence. She could have heartily agreed with that assessment, but she hadn't come here to criticize or lecture. *Jesus, help her to feel Your love through me.*

A quick pain-filled glance, and then Mom asked, "Where's Rem?"

"He's at school. I'll try to bring him by to see you before you get transferred."

"Did you get custody?"

Riley swallowed. Nodded.

Mom pursed her lips. "That's good. I didn't want him going with Doyle. I know you'll do right by him."

"It would be better for him to have two parents that were doing right by him." Riley groaned as soon as the words leapt from her mouth. "I'm sorry, Mom. I really didn't come here to be like that."

Surprisingly, Mom didn't retaliate with a sharp

comeback like Riley expected. Instead, she seemed to deflate. "You're right of course. I've made plenty of mistakes."

Riley squeezed her hands. "We all have, Mom. And we have to live with the consequences of those mistakes. But the good news is Jesus made a way for us not to have to live with the consequences for eternity. And He can give us joy even as we muddle through the results of our actions here on earth."

Mom practically rolled her eyes.

Riley felt her hopes cave in. "Have you read any of the Bible I gave you?"

Mom sighed. "I've looked for joy in lots of places, baby. I can tell you two things for certain. Joy isn't found with a man. And it's not found in a bottle." She shrugged. "And if it's not found there, I highly doubt it's found in religion."

Riley rubbed at a headache pinching her brow. She felt certain that Pastor Mark would have an answer for Mom, but right now Riley couldn't conjure up what that answer might be. Because the truth was, while she knew she was supposed to be filled with joy now that she'd been serving Jesus for awhile, the fact of the matter was that most days it was hard for her to find a lot to smile about. Life was hard. It was one battle after another and, if she was honest, the verses that said things like 'rejoice in the Lord always' mostly had her baffled.

Still, she knew without doubt that giving her life to the Lord was the best thing she'd ever done. He'd given her peace, and she at least had the will to keep fighting the battles, unlike Mom seemed to have.

She eased out a breath. "Mom, I don't have all the answers. I'm just asking you to find a Bible and read it. Can you promise me you'll do that? Maybe go talk to a chaplain a few times?"

Mom's hands were trembling so badly now that her cast rattled against the table. "Guess that's the least I could do for my girl seeing as how I've noticed what a change has taken place in you these past two years. Maybe..." Mom shrugged. "Maybe there is something to this Jesus you keep going on about."

Satisfaction swelled in Riley. Maybe her mom wasn't a lost cause yet.

Mom normally wore a pristine manicure but now she chipped away at more fingernail polish, a sure sign that she was under a lot of stress. "So, who was the guy sitting next to you at the courthouse?"

Riley's mouth went dry at just the mention of Jalen. How did she describe who he was to her? She sorted through a number of words and settled on, "He's a friend, and Rem's soccer coach."

Mom nodded to show she'd heard, but she kept her focus on her nails.

A police officer strode their way. "Time's up."

Riley stood and pulled Mom into an embrace. She didn't care if the officer was right there watching. "I love you, Mom."

Mom couldn't hug her back because of the handcuffs. But she did say. "I love you, too."

Riley let her go.

And as the officer took Mom's arm and led her away, she tossed a look over her shoulder. "Be careful of falling for that man, Riley. Love seems nice on the front side, but it always snakes around to bite you in the end."

Riley stood, forlornly hugging herself in the empty room for a long time. Finally, she took a breath and turned for the door. Mom was probably just speaking from her pain, but it couldn't hurt to take her words as a measure of caution.

Chapter 7

Thursday evening, at Mom's house in the Bluffs, Rem was sitting at the dining room table with his math book, while Riley sat next to him on her laptop looking through real estate websites for the next house she might flip. Happily, Judy Bench, her real estate agent, had called earlier that morning with a serious offer on the one she'd just finished remodeling.

Remington suddenly thrust his math book away and slammed back in his chair, clasping his hands behind his head. "I'll never get this!" The book skidded a good ways on the polished mahogany tabletop.

"What's the matter?" Riley slid the text back towards him.

"It's this algebra!" Remington swiped a disgusted gesture at the book. "A bunch of problems with solve for X this and figure out Y that. How am I supposed to figure out the numbers if they don't give me any? I don't get it!" He slumped forward and dropped his forehead onto folded arms on the table.

Riley grimaced. The problem was, she had never been a math aficionado herself. Still, she pulled the book towards her and glanced at the problems.

The equations on the page seemed to mock her with their indecipherability. She read through the paragraph of instructions at the top of the page. It might as well have been written in Russian for all the good it did her.

She sighed and massaged her temples. "I wish I could help you. But I don't think I'm the best one to ask here."

Rem shot upright and raised his hands above his head dramatically. "Well, I need some help here, Riley! If I fail this class, I'll be the mocking stock of the school!"

Riley snorted, then turned it into a sneeze to hide her amusement at his slaughter of the cliché.

Rem wasn't fooled. He folded his arms. "Whatever."

Still fighting giggles, she covered her mouth.

One corner of his mouth did twitch, but there wasn't much humor in his words when he said, "My life could potentially be over, here, Riley. And all you can do is laugh? I'll get kicked off the soccer team if my grade falls too low!"

Riley squinted her eyes at him. "Let's not go all-drama. I'll find someone to help you."

Remington swept a hand over his head and scratched at the back of his neck. His lips twisted over to one side, and he cast her a quick glance before returning his attention to a spot on the table in front of him. "Thanks. Mom would have told me to just figure it out."

Riley felt all the pain that was wrapped up for her brother in those few words. He had sorrow for what their mother had done, yet a bit of relief that someone was finally taking care of him, and then guilt for the latter. She reached over and ruffled his hair, not having any words to offer. She might be taking care of him better than Mom, but—her focus flickered to the math book—she certainly wasn't enough.

Her mind drifted back to the judge's words from the courtroom. *Every young man needs a father figure in his life.*

She swallowed, doing her best to dispel the image of the first man that came to mind. Even though she'd planned to call him and see if he wouldn't mind spending some time with Rem, she hadn't found the courage to do so yet.

Mom's parting advice in the visitation room had kept replaying in her head each time she thought about dialing his number. *Love seems nice on the front side, but it always snakes around to bite you in the end.*

Despite the fact that she knew Mom's advice came standard with a lot of cynicism, Riley somehow felt Mom's words might have been a nudge from God concurring with the decision Riley had already made. Despite what Jalen thought he wanted, if they jumped into a relationship, she might be enough for him now, but what about down the road? After they'd spent years together and his desire for kids started to outweigh his love for her? What would happen then? That was why it would probably be less painful if they just didn't let this go any further than it already had. And why she needed some time to rebuild her defenses.

Riley knew she needed time to build up her resistance to the man's charms. And by the way her heart was thumping just at the thought of calling him, she *still* needed time. The man's charm held power over her even when he wasn't present!

Straightening, she pondered her other options. *Kylen!* She would just call Kylen and see if he might be able help Rem. Kylen was kind and understanding. A good Christian man, and a police officer, for perfection's sake. He would be the ideal role model for her brother. Surely he wouldn't mind spending a few hours each week helping Remington understand algebra.

She pointed Rem towards the kitchen. "Why don't you see if Lucia has a snack for you, while I make a few quick phone calls? I'll find someone to help. We'll figure this out."

"Fine by me." Remington pushed back from the table and scuffed from the room.

Riley retrieved her phone and dialed Kylen and Taysia's home number. Phone to her ear, she wandered into the living room.

Taysia answered, but it was immediately

apparent that Riley had not called at a good time. In the background Zoe fussed and whimpered, and Taysia seemed a little out of breath.

Riley rubbed her forehead with her fingertips. "Sounds like I'm not calling at the best time. I'm sorry."

"No, no," Taysia said. "This pill is just bringing in another tooth and entirely skipped her nap today. Kylen has been working some long hours lately, and I think she's just missing her daddy. Aren't you pumpkin?" she cooed.

Riley pinched the back of her neck. "Well I think you answered my question before I could even ask it. Remington's having some trouble with his math, and unfortunately I'm not in a position to be able to help him, so I was calling to see if Kylen might be able to, but it sounds like that's not going to be a possibility."

Riley could hear Taysia bouncing Zoe. "Yeah, he's been working twelve-hour days, and I'm not so great with math myself or I'd offer to do it. Still, Kylen might have some time on Sunday afternoons, if that would work for you?"

"No. That's his time to rest. Don't worry about it." Riley scuffed her toe into the plush carpet near the window. "I'll find someone." Zoe started fussing even louder and Riley took pity on her friend. "Listen, I'll let you go. Thanks, and sorry to bother you."

"No problem at all," Taysia said. "Talk soon."

Riley disconnected and stared at her phone

indecisively. She thought of the pastor and the youth pastor and crossed both of them off her mental list. Both men worked full-time jobs in addition to their pastoral duties.

Next she thought of Reece Cahill, but immediately crossed him off as well. The poor man was doing everything he could to keep up with the bed and breakfast his parents had run for years. He was the maintenance man, groundskeeper, and concierge, not to mention full-time father to his adopted daughter Alyssa since his wife Marie worked full time.

Justus came to mind, but Riley was quick to dismiss him. At one time when Remington had been running with the wrong crowd, Justus had been a little hard on him. Which, looking back, was probably exactly what Rem had needed, but she didn't know how her brother would take instruction from him. Not to mention the fact that Justus was newly engaged and busy planning his wedding.

She sighed. Cringed. Flipped through her phone to Jalen's number and simply stared at it for a while. How many times had she listened to that silly message he had left her? *Now you have no excuse not to call me the next time you need something.* It was still stored in her saved list.

And that text he'd sent her... She'd been all geared up to deflect his advances when she left the court house the other day. And then even more so after her visit with Mom. But he hadn't called her even once. He'd only sent one text, Monday evening. *I'm here for you, Riley. Just let me know when you are ready to talk.*

Well... She groaned. She didn't know if she would ever be ready to talk. If she would ever have shored up enough walls around her heart to keep him from slipping back in.

Her eyes fell closed. If she called him and he said he could do it, she would have to be strong, resolute, and determined. Guarded and distant. She would have to put up a wall thicker than the Great Wall of China and stay firmly behind it, keeping him on the other side. Could she be selfless enough to do that?

Remington strode back into the room, munching on a sandwich of some sort. He lifted a brow. "Did you find someone?"

She held up a finger, then punched the green dot on her phone to dial.

Jalen answered on the second ring. "Hello, beautiful."

She felt the pleasure of the compliment all the way to her toes, and despair at her weakness was swift on its heels. She spun away from Remington before he could see the little smile she couldn't seem to withhold.

Stone wall, Riley. Stone wall.

She pinched the bridge of her nose and composed herself. "Jalen listen, how are you at math?"

"Got straight A's all the way through calculus in high school. Why do you ask?"

A breath eased from her. She wasn't sure if it was relief or terror coursing through her. "I was wondering..." She cleared her throat. "Rem is in algebra, and he's having some trouble with some of the concepts. I looked at it, but math was never my strong suit and..."

"Sure I'd be happy to help him."

She closed her eyes. Forced out the words. "That's great. Just a couple hours at first, and then we will see how it goes from there. Does that sound like it would work for you?"

"Sounds fine. Does he need help right now?"

Remington was beside her, nodding his head vigorously. Apparently her volume was up loud enough that he'd been eavesdropping on her conversation.

She pushed her brother back a bit and returned her focus to the call. "Are you available?"

"I am..."

It was the casual way he drawled the words with so much inference that blazed a trail of heat up her neck and into her hair. She slapped a hand to her forehead. "I mean, do you have time right now, to come up? To help Remington with math?"

With only the hint of a chuckle, Jalen graciously returned to the topic at hand. "I can be there in fifteen minutes."

"Thanks." The word was a bit breathy. *Deep inhale.*

"See you soon." He clicked off.

Riley dropped her phone to her side and stared

out the huge floor-to-ceiling windows to the glassy surface of the Pacific. She wondered fleetingly how many years it had taken to build the Great Wall of China, and whether she could accomplish the same task in fifteen minutes.

"Earth to Riley!" Remington waved a hand in front of her face. "Is he coming?"

"Yes. He's on his way."

Remington pumped a fist. "Great, thanks! I'm just going to shoot some hoops until he gets here, alright?"

She nodded her permission.

As soon as Remington stepped out the door to the basketball hoop, Riley decided now was as good a time as any to go talk to Judy Bench, her real estate agent, and see some of the properties she was interested in. She packed up her laptop and mouse and ran up the stairs to her room like the coward she was. She quickly changed into something more comfortable, then slung her purse over her shoulder and hurried down to make her escape before Jalen arrived.

Unfortunately, Lucia had some questions about her shopping list for the next day, which took longer than Riley would have liked.

Knowing she was cutting her escape close, Riley dashed into the garage. Remington had left all three bays wide open and Jalen was already there, shooting hoops with him in the driveway. She jolted to a stop as though she had just run into the very wall she was trying to erect around her heart, then forced herself to casually resume the few steps to her Jeep. Thankfully, Jalen had not parked right behind her.

"Rem, I'm just going to run to town for a couple hours while you and Jalen work." She glanced at her watch. Calculated how far she could stretch Judy Bench's patience and how long it might take Jalen to help Rem with the math, then said, "I'll be home about nine or nine thirty."

Jalen tossed the ball through the hoop and gave Remington a friendly sock to the arm. "Be right back." He turned and jogged her way.

Riley gritted her teeth. *Mental note: Next time just tell Lucia to buy whatever she feels is best!*

She slid into her seat as though she hadn't seen him coming, started the engine, and put the Jeep into 'reverse'.

"Riley." Jalen tapped on her window, a little flash of hurt crossing his features.

Guilt wrapped both fists around her heart and squeezed.

She stomped on the brake, rolled her window down, pressed her lips together, and offered what she hoped was a normal sounding, "Hi."

He rested both palms against her door and leaned down to peer in at her. For a long time, he just studied her in that assessing way of his that set her nerves on edge, and made her aware of every nuance of her expression, and filled her with a desire to spill everything she was feeling to him.

Stone wall, Riley. She turned away and stared

through the windshield at the shovel hanging on the peg board just ahead. "I have to go. I'm meeting my real estate agent in town."

He glanced at the floor between his feet, and nodded like he didn't really believe her. "Going to flip another house?"

She shrugged. "Maybe. If I find the right one."

He tapped the door with the side of his fist and stepped back, folding his arms and remaining silent.

She could probably back out now, but something held her where she was even though his scrutiny made her feel a little bit like an insect under a microscope. She really needed to see if there was a time they could talk. It wasn't fair to keep him hanging and wondering where they stood. "I... Thanks again for coming up to help Rem. It means a lot."

Coward.

She chanced a quick peek at him before zeroing her focus in on a spot on her steering wheel where the leather had cracked a little.

Again, he held his silence. Held it for so long that she finally looked up at him.

He only tilted his head, but a hint of perception crinkled the corners of his eyes, like he might know something he wasn't telling her. Finally he said, "I just wish you didn't feel like you have to run from me."

"I don't!" She was too quick and defensive, and knew it the minute the words left her lips.

One eyebrow lifted. "Don't you?"

She swallowed and clamped her teeth around the rest of the lies that wanted to slip free. Maybe she should just tell him right now that there could never be anything between them? For his own sake. For their future's sake.

But there were so many scenarios to think through. He was Remington's soccer coach, for one. If she broke things off with Jalen, would he take his frustrations with her out on Remington on the soccer field? But after one fleeting consideration, she realized Jalen wasn't the kind of man who would actually do that. Then there was the fact that he was here to help Remington with his math. Would he change his mind if she told him with finality they couldn't ever be together? She wouldn't blame him if he did. But she couldn't see him doing that either. And...

Be fair to him, Riley.

She put the car back into park and angled herself to get a good look at him. "We do need to talk, Jalen."

He lifted his hands in an I-have-all-the-time-in-the-world gesture. "I'm available whenever you are."

Her heart was suddenly pounding so hard she could feel it in her chest. *Not today.* "Can you come for dinner tomorrow?"

He gave a single silent nod.

"Around six?"

"I'll be here."

"Okay. Well, I have to run." She put the car in

reverse once more and backed away, never so relieved and sorrowful at the same time to put some distance between herself and a man.

It was true. She could now verify it. The Great Wall of China could not be built in fifteen minutes.

Chapter 8

If all her wishes for the future were going to come to an end tonight, she might as well make the meal that went along with it memorable.

Riley stepped back and eyed the settings in the formal dining room with a critical eye. She'd taken out all the leaves in the large table to make it smaller, and put Mom's cream crocheted lace tablecloth over a red silk one. The three place settings were laid out with Mom's best cream china with the beautiful cutwork edges. She gave each salad plate another quick straightening and made sure all the silverware was properly lined up along the bottom, exactly one inch from the edge of the table like Dad had always insisted. Lucia had folded the red silk napkins to look like a fleur de lis in the middle of each plate with the gold napkin rings holding each one in place.

Her main debate with herself had been on where she would seat each of them. If she put Rem and Jalen across from each other that would put her sitting right next to Jalen where he might too easily reach over and take her hand. But if she put herself across from him, she would have to put up with his perceptive scrutiny all evening and that might be more than her resolve could handle when it came time to tell him that whatever this was between them could go no further.

She sighed, still unable to decide which seating arrangement might be more damaging. Maybe she would just let the men sit down first and then take the remaining chair.

Her phone chimed from her back pocket. She pulled it out and glanced at the screen. Remington? She frowned and checked the time. She still had twenty minutes before she was due to pick him up from soccer practice. "Hey, Rem. What's up?"

"So...I guess there's this youth group deal going on at church tonight and Keith Tuppins invited me to go. They are doing some bowling thing at the Pin Drop. It's supposed to get over at ten. Is it alright if I go?"

Riley pressed one hand to her forehead and eyed the table set for three.

She'd been counting on Remington to be a buffer for most of the meal. Then she would take five minutes at the end to tell Jalen she couldn't have a relationship with him and rush him out the door and be done with the dreadful task. She really needed Rem here tonight. But how often had she wished he would get more involved with the youth group at church?

She closed her eyes. "Yes. That will be fine. I'll pick you up from the bowling alley at ten then."

"Great." He tried to sound casual, but she could hear the excitement in his voice. "Thanks, Ri."

"Have fun." She hung up and cast a quick glance at the time again. Still over an hour before Jalen was due to arrive.

Her attention drifted to the place settings. Which one to remove? *Criminey!* This was way harder than it needed to be! After another moment's thought she decided that it would be better to be farther away from the man, even if she would have to withstand his soul piercing inspection. She quickly removed the setting at the head of the table, leaving two places across from each other.

Lucia needed to know that Rem wouldn't be here now so she went to the kitchen to inform her, and then made her way upstairs to dress. Why she felt the need to be so formal she wasn't sure. Maybe because it would help her distance herself.

After trying on and tossing aside several dresses, she finally settled on an emerald lace sheath dress with a pair of black low-heeled sandal booties. She paused in front of the full length mirror stand in the corner of her room.

I don't know who you think you are going to impress in that hideous dress. Dad folded his newspaper under his arm and shoved his hands into the pockets of his slacks. Standing by the fireplace, he raked his gaze over her where she'd stopped on the bottom step.

Riley tipped up her chin and refused to let him see that the words had hurt. She wouldn't give him the satisfaction. Besides, it was the night of her first prom and she didn't want to ruin her makeup. Still, she swept a palm over the custom watered-silk sapphire gown that she and Mom had spent hours on with the seamstress. She loved the feel of the silk beneath her fingers. The swish of the soft material around her ankles. The swath of tiny diamonds that graced the neckline and hem.

Nonsense, Dylan! Mom rushed toward her, arms outstretched and a reassuring look on her face, even if there was a slight wobble in her step. *She looks lovely. This dress is the latest fashion, and I might add, it cost you a fortune.* Mom cast him a gently chastising look.

But Dad only pulled out his paper and went back to reading the financial section. *No amount of money can turn a chicken into a peacock.*

Riley blinked and refocused on herself in the present. Yeah, she might not win any beauty pageants—

She tore her thoughts from that path and purposely focused on words Dakota had drilled into her. She could almost hear Dakota even now admonishing her to say the verses when she was falling back into the lies of her past. "Out loud, Riley, let me hear them."

Riley spoke to herself in the mirror the words from The Message version of First Corinthians 5. "Our firm decision is to work from this focused center: One man died for everyone. That puts everyone in the same boat. He included everyone in his death so that everyone could also be included in his life, a resurrection life, a far better life than people ever lived on their own. Because of this decision we don't evaluate people by what they have or how they look. We looked at the Messiah that way once and got it all wrong, as you know. We certainly don't look at him that way anymore. Now we look inside, and what we see is that anyone united with the Messiah gets a fresh start, is created new. The old life is gone; a new life burgeons!"

Riley took a deep breath and gave herself an encouraging nod. The dress and shoes would do.

By the time she'd freshened her makeup and done her hair, Jalen was set to arrive within minutes. She would just run down and see if Lucia needed anything before he got here.

She was on the way down the stairs when her phone rang. It was Dad.

Think of the devil. Remorse immediately gripped her for the thought. *Jesus, forgive me. Help me to let it go.*

Why would he be calling? Everything in her

stilled. Dad never called. Whatever this was, it wasn't going to be good, she could feel it.

Instead of going to the kitchen, she stepped out onto the deck and leaned on the rail. "Hi, Dad." The breeze tugged at her updo.

"Riley, listen." He went straight to business, as usual. "My attorney and I have filed the paperwork to cut off your mother's alimony. It will only take a few days to go through. The paperwork is just a formality really. I won't continue supporting her when she insists on throwing her life away like this."

Riley's eyes dropped closed. Without the alimony money, she would not be able to keep Mom's house running. The house was paid for, but the property taxes on the large estate were exorbitant, not to mention other expenses. Worst of all she wouldn't be able to afford the salary payments.

She propped her forehead into her palm. "Dad, without that money I won't be able to pay Lucia and Roddy. I'll have to let them go."

A snort burst through the earpiece. "If they have any smarts at all, they saw this coming a long time ago."

Riley blinked back tears. Lucia and Roddy had worked for them since before she was born. "How can you be so callous, Dylan?" The old tendency to disrespect him by using his given name when she was angry came much too easily. She literally clamped her teeth on her tongue before she could say anything more she might regret.

"I see not much has changed," Dad grated. "You're still as insolent as ever."

Regret washed through her. For two years she'd been trying to show her father that her life had changed because of her relationship with the Lord and with one sentence she'd just undone all her hard work. "I'm sorry, Dad. You're right. I shouldn't have said that."

A moment of ringing silence hung between them, and then he must have decided to let it go because he moved on with, "This is nothing personal, Riley. It's just business."

Business. The people her father had known the longest and cared for the deepest had become simply numbers on a spreadsheet to him in the last few years.

She sighed. "What about Rem?"

"Well, I take it you are his legal guardian now?"

Would he even care if she wasn't? If the courts had give his son over to his money-grubbing brother? The tears spilled over. "Yes, I am."

"We'll start sending his child support checks to you, then, instead of to Katherine."

"That's fine." Riley gave him her PO box number in town.

"Good. Alright then." Dead air indicated he'd hung up without so much as a goodbye.

Riley didn't move. She didn't even know how much he sent each month for the support of his son. But maybe between that and her paycheck she would be able to keep the house for Mom until she got out. Keep Lucia and Roddy in work.

Her mind flashed to the money Dad had given her when he kicked her out of the house when she turned eighteen. Maybe it was time to start using some of that for other things than flipping houses.

Her teeth clenched together. She still got so angry every time she thought of that stupid money. Being beholden to her father was the last thing on earth she wanted.

She released a breath. "We'll get it figured out, Dad."

Why was she still talking to him when he wasn't even there? She plunked the phone onto the rail next to her and let her fingers massage some of the tension from her forehead. She wanted to add, "Not that you care," but managed to restrain herself.

She needed to get back inside. She turned for the house and gasped. Jalen was standing on the deck next to the slider, hands slipped into his pockets. He tilted his head toward the living room. "Sorry. Lucia let me in and told me you were out here."

Riley dashed at the telltale moisture beneath her eyes.

Jalen stepped closer. Concern pinched his features as his gaze darted between her and her phone. "You okay?"

She waved away his worry and tried to brush by him and slip through the slider.

But he caught her wrist, his fingers gentle and

tantalizing. "Talk to me, Ri."

The warmth of his palm on her forearm and the probing of his brown eyes had her heart hammering in her throat. In that moment she would have given anything to have the freedom to throw herself into his arms and tell him all about her heartache. But somehow she managed to dredge up the reason she'd asked him here tonight, so instead, she twisted her arm free and backed away a step, folding her arms around herself. "It's nothing really. Just my father being my father. I'll figure it out."

Jalen gave a nod. "All on your own, huh?"

The words contained a lot more understanding than they ought to since she hadn't given him her planned speech on why they couldn't be together yet.

He looked down and scuffed the toe of his black dress shoe at a knot on the deck. "Every burden is a lot lighter if you share it with someone who cares, Riley." He looked back up at her, but in his gaze there was the dull sheen of pain. He knew why she'd asked him here. She could see it.

She steeled herself. Looked away. "Some burdens are meant to be carried alone, Jalen."

How had the conversation so quickly morphed away from her father's phone call? She needed to get them back on track.

She lifted her phone to draw his attention to it. "My father filed to cut off alimony. Without that money…" She swept a gesture over the house and grounds. "I won't be able to keep this going. Lucia and Roddy have worked for us since before I was born. This is all Mom has." She batted away the conversation before her tears started in earnest. "Like I said, I'll figure it out."

"On your own." It was a statement this time.

Why was he pushing the issue? She clenched her jaw. Dipped her head once in acknowledgement.

He drew near slowly, like a rescuer approaching a skittish animal.

She should step away. Maybe put the patio table between them, but her shoes seemed to be cemented to the deck. Her breaths came rapid and shallow.

He'd worked his curls into a casually mussed spike. His dark eyes had impossibly long thick lashes, and his right eyebrow had a tiny scar through it on the outside edge. Each detail of his features became more distinct the closer he came. He was freshly shaven, but his stubble was so black it still left an observable line along his angular jaw and upper lip. His lips were full and soft, and currently tensed with a bit of aggravation. She remembered how firm and controlled they had been when he kiss—

Her eyes widened when she realized where her thoughts were taking her and she dragged her gaze to the knot of his tie in the hopes of breaking some of his hold on her.

Jalen stopped right in front of her, his hands still in his pockets pushing open the gray-blue of his suit jacket which angled out to emphasize his broad sturdy shoulders. Today he wore a honey-gold shirt with a blue and gold floral tie. The man was way too handsome for her good.

She swallowed and tore her attention down to her phone where she picked at the rubber of her case.

Slowly, one of Jalen's hands pulled from his pocket and he lifted it to touch her chin, urging her to look at him once more. He dipped his head when he had her attention. "You made one mistake by staying with a guy who didn't love you, Ri. Don't make another by pushing away one who does."

She drew in a breath, feeling the shock of those words all the way to her core. "You can't love me." She took a step back.

His mouth twitched and he scooped a hand through his dark curls and clutched the back of his neck. "Can't I?"

A tremor started deep inside her. The last thing she wanted was to hurt this man who had given her so much. And based on his expression right now, she knew that was exactly what she was doing. If only she had never let him close in the first place.

He stepped away quickly then and thrust his hand into his pocket. He strode to the rail and put his back to her, bouncing on his toes a couple times. "Look at the view from up here, Riley."

She scanned the strip of beach far below, the large rocks that broke the surface of the waves along this stretch of the shore, and the gulls that soared in circles drifting on currents of air. The patches of bright pink and yellow wild flowers that dotted the rocky parts of the shore. It was a magnificent view, but she couldn't put her finger on what he was getting at. "Yes, it's beautiful."

He spun to face her, leaned his back into the rail, and crossed one leg in front of the other. He jingled something in his pocket, maybe his keys, but his focus drilled into her. "From what you've said you're determined to figure this out on your own, but if you *were* to ask me, I'd remind you that you have a really big place here." He tipped a nod to the sprawling house behind her. "I'd tell you that lots of people would be happy to pay rent for a room in a place like this, and that the rent might cover enough costs to let you keep going."

Cool air swept into her mouth and she realized her jaw had dropped open. She snapped it shut and swallowed. That was actually a really good idea. And it would keep her from having to use Dad's money.

There was way too much room here for her and Remington alone. And with Dakota and Justus getting married soon, she probably would be moving up here permanently anyhow. Why not as the landlord? But...she had questions.

She swallowed her pride. "And if I were to ask you...what would you say to do about shared bathrooms and laundry facilities? State laws? Rental agreements?"

Lucia poked her head out the sliding door.

"Dinner is ready, Miss Riley."

"Thank you, Lucia. We'll be right in." But when Lucia stepped back into the house and slipped the door shut behind her neither of them moved. Riley looked at him, her questions still hanging between them.

Jalen's features softened. And a smile started at the corners of his eyes before it spread to his mouth. "How about we go in and talk about it over dinner?" He straightened. "I like that topic a lot better than the one you really asked me here to discuss."

Chapter 9

Jalen pushed back from the table and laid the red silk napkin he hadn't dared to use next to his empty plate. "Everything was delicious, Riley. Thank you."

Over the course of the meal he'd answered every question he could about rentals and state laws. And part way through she'd jumped up to grab a notebook so she could jot down notes.

But now that the meal was over and Riley had told Lucia she could bring in the coffee and dessert, he could see the change of topic coming. She wasn't giving up on her mission to boot him out of her life. He felt the pain of it just below his sternum.

She was bent over the notebook on the pretense of skimming her notes, but he could sense her gathering her courage.

Beautiful had always been a word he would have used to describe her, even the broken beauty she had sported when he'd first met her years ago, but the word was especially apropos tonight. The green lace of her dress drew his attention to the golden highlights in the upsweep of her red hair, and emphasized the amber flecks in the depths of her irises. His only complaint was that she'd somehow done away with her freckles, and he missed them. She inhaled long and slow, nibbling on her lower lip, and he could tell she wasn't really seeing the words she was staring at.

Lucia came in and set some sort of chocolate concoction in a fluted cup before each of them along with a cup of coffee. She set cream and sugar on the table and then stepped back. "Will there be anything else, Miss Riley?"

Riley jolted from her reverie and lifted her head. "No. Thank you, Lucia. This will be fine." She lifted her spoon and he saw her hand tighten around it. "Jalen listen..." She twirled the utensil through the dollop of whipped cream on her bowl.

He lifted his own spoon and tasted the dessert without really tasting it. *Lord, I need a little strength here. Give me the right words.*

Her throat worked. "You've always been more than kind to me. And I care about you a lot. I really do. But there are...*reasons* why I can never let anything more develop between us."

She paused and her gaze flickered to him for the briefest of seconds, but he wanted to hear her out before he stated his case so he held his silence.

Her focus returned to the now mangled mound of whipped cream, her cheeks pinking brightly. "I'm sorry about the other night."

Their kiss. His stomach tightened.

"You just caught me a little off guard and I shouldn't have let—I mean it was nice..." Her neck turned even redder.

And his stomach relaxed as his hopes soared.

"But I shouldn't have..." She cleared her throat. "Well, I just need you to trust me when I say there can be nothing more between us."

"No." Even he was taken aback by the abruptness of the word, quiet though it was.

She blinked and looked over at him.

He pushed his chair back just enough that he could lean forward and plant his elbows onto his knees and look into her face very closely across the table. "You want to end things between us before they even get started? I think you owe me an explanation for why you want to do that, don't you?"

She swallowed and this time her face paled. Her fingers rose to stroke the hollow at the base of her throat.

His heart went out to her. But he wasn't going to let her off the hook so easily. "It's just me, Ri. Talk to me. Was it something I said? Something I did?"

"No!" She shook her head. "No, nothing like that."

He eased out a breath he didn't know he'd been holding. "So? What?"

She couldn't seem to look him in the face. Or find her voice.

That was okay. He'd outwaited many a juvenile

delinquent. He could outwait one stubborn woman. He picked up his dessert and his spoon and savored the delicate silky chocolate as he gave her time to make the next move. He finished and still she hadn't spoken. Neither had she touched her dessert. He folded his hands across his chest and leaned back, content to simply watch her all evening.

Finally she tossed her spoon down and daggered him a look.

Riley was about to lay out the full gamut of her broken life and why he didn't want to be with a woman like her, but both of their phones rang at the same moment. She might have let it go to voicemail, but when she glanced down, it was Dakota's smiling face on her screen.

Jalen glanced over, lifting his phone. "It's Justus."

Her heart squeezed as she pointed to her screen. "This is Dakota."

In unison they made the decision and both answered.

"Hi Dakota." Riley plugged her free ear so she could fully concentrate. She held her breath wondering if there was an emergency.

"Riley, are you busy right now?"

"Uh..." Riley lifted her gaze to see what Justus might have been calling Jalen about. If Jalen needed to leave, she would be free too. Dakota's voice sounded a little nervous like something might be wrong.

Jalen spoke into his phone. "Give me a sec." Removing the phone from his ear he pressed it to his chest and spoke to her. "Justus wants to know if I can come down to Dakota's place."

"And Dakota wants to know if I'm busy."

Jalen's lips twitched speculatively.

Riley lowered her voice. "Do you think they eloped? And want to tell us?"

Jalen shrugged in his signature no-extra-words manner.

She suddenly saw her way out of having to give him the full truth. Maybe if she just left things as they were he'd eventually accept that they couldn't be together.

Excuse though it was, and despite the fact that she really should make sure he fully understood, she grabbed on to it like a lifeline. Tonight had been nice, up until he'd been so difficult about breaking things off. Why couldn't the man just walk away and leave her to lick her wounds in peace.

She glanced at the time. There were still several hours before she needed to pick Remington up from the bowling alley. "So do you want to go down?"

He spread his hands leaving the decision up to her, the question over their unfinished discussion still lingering in his expression.

That did it. She lifted her phone back to her ear. "Dakota? I can be there in fifteen minutes."

"Oh great! See you then!" Dakota clicked off without giving even a hint of what the gathering was about.

"Did Justus tell you what's going on?" she asked as Jalen rose and pulled her chair out for her. The gesture made her heartbeat quicken. Not even her father who'd been fastidious about the way he treated his women in public had ever held her chair for her.

"No," he said.

Riley hurried into the kitchen and informed Lucia that she and Jalen would be leaving now. Riley squeezed her around the shoulders. "I don't know what time I'll be home, so don't wait up."

Lucia had her head in the depths of the fridge and was muttering to herself in her usual way when Riley stepped through the door into the garage.

Jalen was waiting for her. "Want to ride with me?"

Despite the recent reprieve she'd given herself, Riley knew she didn't dare let him get too close again.

She held up her keys. "I'd better drive myself. I have to get Rem at ten, and then you won't have to drive us all the way up here before you head out to your room at Serenity Shores."

He pursed his lips and didn't look too happy about it, but it only took him a moment to nod his agreement. "Alright. See you down there."

The house Riley and Dakota had rented together

for several years was on a dead end street on the northwest end of Marinville.

Riley arrived only moments after Jalen did. He was swinging his suit coat on as she pulled up behind him at the curb and shut off her engine. He came over and opened her door, holding out a hand to help her down.

"Thanks." On the pretense of smoothing her dress, she let go of his hand as soon as her feet were solidly on the street.

But Jalen had somehow managed to trap her between her Jeep, her door, and himself. He had one arm propped on the door and the other propped on the hardtop. His gaze slid the length of her before rebounding to her eyes. "I never told you how beautiful you look tonight. My only complaint is"—he tapped the end of her nose—"I miss your freckles."

Her nose wrinkled at just the mention of the brown spots that had plagued her all her life.

He chuckled, but still had not moved. His head tipped to one side and a glitter of something more serious touched his brown irises. "Don't ever let anyone make you feel like you aren't perfect just the way you were created, Riley."

Heart hammering, she pulled in a slow breath. Heaven's mercy, she wanted to take the one small step that separated them and kiss him right then and there. She clutched her small purse tightly in both hands and propped her back against the side of her Jeep's driver's seat to keep herself from following through.

He leaned close. "Whatever is going on, we can make it through it. Together, if you are willing. And if you're not, I'll have to honor that. But for now, I'm afraid I've decided not to let you push me away unless you give me a superb reason, Riley."

The words could have sent a jolt of fear through her, after all she'd known men who wouldn't take no for an answer all her life. But with Jalen, there was no threat to the words, only an underlying determination that somehow warmed her despite the goose bumps it raised along the back of her neck. Stubborn man, why did he demand an explanation? He should just accept her wishes because she didn't know if she had any reasons that would be good enough for him. And that was what she was afraid of.

She needed space and she had no words right now. She stiff-armed him out of her way and strode a few paces to put some distance between them.

Riley noticed that Reece's big blue truck was already parked in the driveway. Just then Kylen and Taysia pulled up behind Riley's Jeep in their restored red Mustang.

Kylen and Taysia climbed out, grinning. "Do any of us know why we are here?" Taysia asked.

Jalen had shut her Jeep's door and now caught up to Riley. He put one hand to the small of her back and started them all toward the house. "Guess we'll all know soon enough."

Riley clenched her hands against the enticing

feel of his guiding touch.

She stepped out quickly. "Where's my Zoe?" she asked Taysia over her shoulder.

"Oh, Kylen's parents have her tonight."

"Which is why we were able to drop everything and come when Justus and Dakota called us a few minutes ago." Kylen rolled down the sleeves of his dress shirt and buttoned his cuffs as they walked.

Jalen rang the bell, and Justus answered the door with a huge grin on his face, but didn't say anything before leading them all into the living room. The room only had a loveseat and two arm chairs. Reece and Marie were already in the loveseat. Kylen took one of the armchairs and pulled Taysia onto his lap.

Jalen's attention skimmed over the single remaining chair, then over Kylen and Taysia, before he gave Riley a hint of a wicked grin.

Riley felt her face heat at the insinuation. And it had a lot less to do with embarrassment than the fact that she knew she would enjoy snuggling up with the man.

But after only a split second, he motioned for her to take the remaining chair.

As soon as Riley sank into the seat, Jalen propped one hip onto an arm of her chair and settled in like he planned to be there for awhile. The tantalizing scent of his cologne wafted to her.

She clenched her teeth. No doubt about it, she was a terrible wall builder.

Across from them, Marie snuggled into Reece's

side and rested one hand on his chest. Next to them in the other armchair, Taysia leaned back against Kylen's chest and settled her head onto his shoulder. At the end of the room Dakota practically bounced up and down. Justus stepped up behind Dakota, bent forward and dropped a kiss onto her hair. Dakota leaned back against him, and clasped the arms he slipped around her, a big sloppy grin splitting her face.

Feeling most conspicuous, Riley tucked her hands beneath her legs and ducked her head. Nothing like being in a room full of happy couples with a man you were trying to resist.

Jalen propped his elbow into the seatback above her head, leaned close and spoke low. "Did you know your ears turn the prettiest shade of pink when you are embarrassed?"

Riley felt the burn she hadn't previously noticed. She shrugged, doing her best to look innocent. "Must have gotten a little sun out on the deck today."

"That's the best you've got?" There was warm humor in the question.

She squirmed and scooted as close to the opposite arm from Jalen as she could.

At the other end of the room, Justus cleared his throat to gather everyone's attention.

"Okay, so here's the deal," Dakota said. She peeked over her shoulder at Justus who only seemed to have eyes for her. "Justus and I have waited two years to be able to get married. And we just decided...well...that we don't want to wait any longer. But we didn't want to elope and not have all our friends at the ceremony. So..." She spread her hands. "You guys willing to be the witnesses to our wedding tonight?"

"Tonight?" several of them gasped in unison.

Dakota and Justus laughed, gave each other a quick kiss, and then nodded.

Justus leaned forward and rested his chin on Dakota's shoulder. "Out on the beach. Pastor is going to meet us there at seven thirty."

Riley glanced at the time on her phone. "That's in thirty minutes!"

They both nodded.

"But what about your parents?" Riley asked Dakota.

If Riley had parents who loved her the way Dakota's loved her, she wouldn't want them to miss her wedding for a second.

Dakota snuggled her head into Justus's shoulder. "I called them and told them what we were going to do. They won't be home for two more years. We'll do an anniversary celebration with them when they get here."

"But Dakota you need to have a pretty dress!" Taysia protested.

Dakota smiled serenely. "I bought one this morning."

"Do you have a marriage license?" That from Kylen.

Riley grinned. Of course the lawman in the

group would think of the legal side of things.

Dakota laughed. "Oh trust me, we have one. The greater part of our day has been spent at the court house."

Justus chuckled and pumped his eyebrows. "There's supposed to be a three day waiting period. But we paid the extra fee to waive that and the woman at the courthouse was not happy to have to do the extra work for us."

"Well come on, girl." Marie was on her feet and nudging Justus away from Dakota and pushing Dakota down the hallway. "Let's go get you dressed for your wedding!"

Taysia jumped to her feet too. "You guys take Justus to the beach after he dresses and we girls will bring Dakota along as soon as she's ready."

"This eloping thing has potential, don't you think?" Jalen teased for her ears alone.

Riley lurched from her seat and hurried after the other women, at the same moment relieved and reluctant to leave Jalen's gentle teasing behind. Hoping the heat in her face would be gone by the time they all got to Dakota's room, she trailed Taysia down the hall.

How had he dodged her planned break-up speech and turned the night into one where he was teasing her about eloping? And she liked it! Oh how the man had her muddled!

She stepped into the trill of happy conversation in Dakota's room and forced her thoughts to the present.

With deft movements, Marie helped an almost glowing Dakota into the dress she had purchased. Dakota eyed herself in the full length mirror with a bit of awe in her expression, and Riley blinked back tears of happiness for her friend. Marie and Taysia fussed and fluffed over Dakota's dress and her hair and her makeup, but Riley was content to sit back and just soak in the experience.

She'd known the future held only happiness for Dakota and Justus, from way back in the beginning of their relationship. How many nights had she lain awake in her room and listened to the low murmur of Dakota skyping with Justus? How many times had she rested a hand over her womb and known there could never be a relationship like theirs for her?

And she'd been content to deal with that—until Jalen had come back to town.

"Riley, are you crying?" Marie peered into her face.

Riley dashed at the moisture and stepped over to bend down and one-arm-squeeze Dakota where she sat before her vanity mirror. "I'm just so happy for you guys!"

It was true. She really was happy for them. And if her tears were partly a pity party, well, they didn't need to know about it.

Dakota hugged her back. "There's going to be a great guy for you someday too, Riley." A gleam leapt into her gaze. "In fact, maybe he's here, already?"

Oh no. They were not going there!

Riley ignored the last question. "Well, today is about you and not me. Now come on, let us look at you." She took Dakota's hand and helped her off of the stool.

The sleeveless dress with the empire waist that Dakota had chosen was the perfect gown for a beach wedding. A swath of ecru lace banded Dakota's ribs, and from there a series of sheer white pleats flowed, seeming to lift on a breeze with each step she took. A sheath of white silk formed the underdress.

"Oh! You look beautiful!" Marie gushed.

"Thanks." Dakota hugged Taysia first. And then Marie.

Then she turned and pulled Riley into her embrace. Dakota hung on to Riley a little longer than she had the others before setting her back at arm's length. "You've been an amazing roomy!"

Riley squeezed her hands. "So have you! And now you and Justus will get to stay here together."

Dakota tilted her head. "Will that leave you in a bind if you have to move out of your mom's place?"

Riley tucked an escaped wisp of hair behind her ear. She hadn't shared with any of them yet about her father's decision to cut off alimony, but with Jalen's reminder that she could rent part of the place out, she knew they were going to be able to keep the house. "We are going to be fine. I'm considering renting part of it out."

"Oh! That's a fabulous idea!"

Taysia, ever the organizer, was shooing them all

towards the door.

"Yes, come on," Marie added, scooping up a large jeweled barrette and a cream silk ribbon from the vanity. "We have to stop by Thrift and Save to grab a bouquet or two that I can tweak into a nosegay right quick on our way out to the beach!"

Dakota's tinkling laughter drifted down the hallway. "I'm so glad my girls have my back!"

Riley reached for her keys. "I'll drive." Her Jeep might never carry another bride, but for tonight there would be one bright eyed, utterly glowing one riding to her wedding in it.

Chapter 10

Jalen clasped the wrist of one hand in the palm of the other and settled his feet comfortably into the sand. The weather was cooperating beautifully for Justus and Dakota's ceremony. And at seven thirty, the sun was just dipping below the horizon.

Clutching a tightly bound bouquet of red roses and yellow sunflowers, Dakota walked through the last rose-hued sunbeams to Justus's side. The man looked like he could be knocked over with one finger.

Jalen bit back a grin. And then he looked over at Riley, standing there with the dusk-dimmed rays of the sun creating a halo in her upswept hair. Barefooted, with her shoes lying beside her, and her pink toenails curling in and out of the golden sand, she smoothed her hands over her green lace dress and smiled wistfully at the couple standing before them. That smile of hers made his pulse do crazy things, and he realized his expression just might mirror Justus's.

Jalen transferred his attention to the sand in front of him and tried to focus on what the reverend was saying about the sanctity of the union between man and woman.

He wished he'd held back. Hadn't pushed her. If he hadn't kissed her so soon maybe she wouldn't be running so hard, right now. Except...he could hardly find it in himself to regret that kiss.

But it had hurt a lot worse than he'd expected to hear her say they couldn't be together. To have her drawing into herself like a turtle slowly receding into its shell.

When the minister pronounced, "May I present to you Mr. and Mrs. Justus Teague", and everyone whooped and clapped, Jalen realized he'd let his mind wander again.

Justus and Dakota gave out hugs all around, faces beaming with little intimate smiles just for each other.

Jalen waited until everyone else had offered their congratulations before he approached and clapped Justus on the shoulder. He wondered if they were going to be able to have a honeymoon since they'd rushed so quickly into things. "Are you two going to get to run off somewhere together?"

Dakota started to say, "Well with my job—"

"—Actually, yes." Justus grinned at Dakota with great satisfaction. "I talked to Dakota's boss and we have two weeks off. We are leaving tonight for Portland, and then tomorrow we fly out to... Well, that's my secret." He pumped his eyebrows at his bride.

"Justus..." Dakota melted against him with a dreamy expression that left no question that she'd love to be alone with her husband right at that moment.

Jalen could take a hint. He clapped Justus on the shoulder once more. "Well, you two have a good trip." He didn't even think Justus heard him. He made his way across the sand to where the rest of the wedding party was sitting on a long driftwood log admiring the now crimson sunset.

Riley sat alone off to one side, slightly away from the other two couples. He eased down beside her.

"It was a nice ceremony," she said, not taking her attention off the horizon.

He didn't want to admit that he'd had a hard time keeping focused on anything but her, so he only nodded. "Yeah."

"Dakota was a beautiful bride."

He made a noncommittal noise. He'd barely looked at anyone but Riley. Just like right now. She watched the changing colors of the sky, he watched her.

She wiggled a little on the log. "You're staring."

"Mmhmm."

Her teeth captured her upper lip in a nervous gesture, and he felt sure if the dusk wasn't obscuring it, he'd be able to see a telltale pink blush. "You have no idea how beautiful you are, do you?"

She flashed him a surprised look before honing

her focus into the fabric near her knee. "Jalen, listen..."

Now he'd gone and done it. Pushed her too quickly again. She was like a skittish doe, and he needed to remember that. If he wanted her to feel comfortable around him, he had to keep quiet. Go slow. Offer nothing but time and patience.

The problem was that after waiting for her for two years, he was more than ready to advance their relationship. She obviously was not.

He spoke before she could find the words she seemed to be searching for. "I'm sorry, Riley. I didn't mean to offend."

She shook her head. "No. You didn't. It's fine."

Okay... He cupped the back of his neck and pondered, feeling a little lost as to what he might be doing wrong here. Maybe she just needed more time to get to know him. Time as just friends.

He eased out a breath and took another risk. "Riley, ever since we met two years ago, I've been biding my time. Waiting for the day when you might be ready for another relationship. I know what you said at dinner, but I meant what I said by your Jeep earlier. I'm asking you to give us a chance. Don't shut me out before we even get some time to get to know each other. Unless I'm not a guy you can see yourself with and you've just been trying to let me down easy?"

She looked at him, her expression soft and concerned. "Jalen, it's not that."

A breath of relief shot from his lungs. "I can feel

your fear, Ri. And I don't want to do anything to hurt you. So if I've made you uncomfortable in some way—"

Her hand settled over his, sealing off any further words. "You haven't made me uncomfortable."

He turned his hand and captured her fingers. They were cool and soft. Slender. "So what is it then?"

She tilted her head as though considering her answer, but didn't speak.

The last shards of crimson on the glassy sea of the Pacific faded into a dull pink, and then a dusky gray. The never ceasing sound of the waves, and the whispering of the evening breeze in the beach grass, created a symphony with the croaking of a frog, and the chirping of a cricket.

Jalen was content to give her the time she needed to form an answer. Sitting there holding her hand, he thought he might be content to sit there forever if she would just give him a chance and not walk away.

Finally, she let a long sigh escape, and he felt a shiver course through her. Quietly he pulled off his suit jacket and draped it around her shoulders, hoping that wouldn't disturb her deliberation or the tranquility that had settled around them.

As he eased back she looked over at him, and there were tears shimmering in her eyes. "You're so patient with me Jalen. I don't deserve a guy like you."

A rock settled into the pit of his stomach. He

stood, straddled the log, and then sat again, scooting closer to her to have a good gage on her expression in the rapidly falling darkness. "Riley Ross, nothing could be further from the truth."

She kept her face averted, stubbornly staring out over the waves.

"Look at me. Please?" He slipped one hand beneath her chin and nudged her face toward him. Once she gave in, he cupped her face in both hands to ensure he had her full attention. "You deserve to be loved in the most tender and most patient of ways. You deserve to have your thoughts heard, no matter how long it takes you to formulate them. You deserve a love one hundred times better than I'll ever be able to give you. But I hope"—he gave her a quick little grin that turned immediately serious again—"that you'll settle for me."

Her face contorted. "Jay, you'd be the one settling."

He shook his head, wishing he could crack open his emotions and let her feel even a fraction of his love for her. Or maybe that he could go back in time and thrash on the guy who had stripped from her the truth of her self-worth. "Nothing could be further from the truth, Ri. Nothing."

She tilted her head and dropped a kiss against his palm. "You're good for me, Jalen Rivera."

His heart soared as though it had just been catapulted from a slingshot. But he tried for a casual, "Don't I know it!"

She sniffed. Rolled her eyes. Swiped at her

cheeks.

He pressed his luck. "So I happen to know that you can't get Rem till ten, and I also happen to know that you love your chocolate. I hear that the Marinville Chocolate Shop has some pretty amazing truffles." He offered his most charming smile and laid the words on her. "I promise to be on my best behavior. For tonight."

A puff of released air seemed to deflate her. "Jalen...I shouldn't."

Knife to the chest. He'd thought he was making progress. "Why not?"

Her thumbnail went into her mouth. "Because I might like it too much."

Hope sprang eternal. Knife at least partially extracted from chest. "And that would be a bad thing?"

"Yes." The word was barely a wisp of air.

This had to mostly be good, right?

He rubbed his jaw and tried for some humor. "Alright, I'm willing to work with you on this. I promise to make any time you spend with me as miserable as possible to help you avoid that possibility."

A soft giggle escaped, sending his heart rate soaring into the stratosphere. She looked at him then. And not even a sucker punch from a world heavyweight champion could have knocked the air out of him so effectively.

Her eyes were soft and luminous in the nearly absent light. "What am I going to do with you, Jalen

Rivera?"

He swallowed and offered a hopeful, "Have a truffle with me?"

The battle was still waging inside her. He could see the effects of it on her face. And he saw the moment she gave in, too. She bent and hooked the sandals near her feet, letting them dangle from two fingers as she stood. "Forthwith to the Marinville Chocolate Shop, oh king of my misery!"

Jalen leapt up, feeling in that moment like he just might be able to conquer the world. "Aye, my lady, and I vow a torturous experience awaits." He motioned for her to precede him across the sand.

Her chuckle did his heart good.

Cautiously he asked, "So have I talked you out of sending me packing?" So much hung on her answer, he could feel his pulse thrumming in his veins.

And then she nodded, ever so slightly. "For now."

He might have hoped for something a little more emphatic, but he would take what he could get and be thankful for it.

Still, something uneasy lingered at the back of his mind. He couldn't quite pin it down. But if it wasn't something he had said or done why did she feel the need to push him away?

Chapter 11

The next Tuesday was the boys' first soccer game. Riley pulled her Jeep to a stop in the parking lot and frowned miserably at the rain sluicing from the sky in sheets.

Her brother better know how much she loved him to come and stand for nearly two hours in the pouring rain for him. Grunting, she grabbed up her gloves, rain poncho, and umbrella. She left the cushioned seat she'd just bought from the high school glee club where it lay. She would only get soaked clean through if she tried to sit on the uncovered, grooved metal bleachers with this rain coming down. She'd just have to stand and hope that the wind didn't slant the rain too far sideways.

As she climbed from the car she twisted her mouth in derision. Who was she kidding? She was going to be soaked and freezing by the time this game was over.

Her path to the home team's section took her right past the players huddled beneath some popup shelters. Jalen was wearing a dark blue suit today with a lighter blue shirt and matching tie.

Oh man! She cringed for him. What happened to a business suit when it got soaked? Hopefully, his was made of something that wasn't going to be ruined by the weather.

He was speaking to his team. Focused. Intense. Pacing.

"Alright guys, listen up. We aren't going to moan and complain about the rain. This is soccer! We're bigger men than that. I want you all to go out there and play hard, play fair, play for a well deserved win. I hear anyone cussing and I'll pull you out and you'll sit for the rest of the game, understood? No one talks back to the ref. He makes a call and you say, 'Yes sir, Mr. Ref, sir.'"

One of the boys raised his hand.

Jalen acknowledged him with a nod.

"Do we really have to say that?"

The whole team busted up laughing and a couple kids closest to the questioner punched him in the shoulder. "'Course not, you knucklehead."

Jalen smiled but snapped his fingers to regain the team's attention. "My point is, Regan" —he pinned the boy who'd asked the question with a look—"that I want you to be respectful gentlemen out there, got it?"

"Yes, sir!" the team chorused.

Jalen looked up directly at her then, and she realized she'd come to a stop just outside the popup shelter in order to eavesdrop on his pregame pep talk. He gave her a bold wink that sent a ripple of amusement through the team, and she felt her embarrassment blazing a trail up her neck.

She gave him a quick nod, and hurried forward toward the other spectators.

"Alright boys," she heard him say, "it's go time. Starters get out there on the field."

Riley felt a lot of pride in Rem's hard work when she noticed that he was one of the first players out onto the field. Rain already splashed up from the turf with each step he took and his hair was plastered to his head.

She cringed. At least she got to stand under the relative shelter of her umbrella through the worst of this storm. Poor Rem was going to be a prune by the time this game was over.

The ref blew the whistle and the game was underway.

Riley's gaze wandered to Jalen striding a short path from one side of the popup shelter to the other. His attention was focused on his team and he was already giving the players instructions. "Johnny, drop back a bit. Kent, be a wall out there, nothing gets past you, now. Nothing! That's my man! Nice steal. Look up! Look up!"

Riley's stomach turned over in a slow curl. This was a man any woman could happily spend the rest of her life with. A true encourager. A motivator. A listener.

And she was a selfish coward for not letting him go.

The other night she should have just cut their ties. Told him he wasn't the kind of man she could be interested in, and been done with it. But there had been so much pain laced in his question. And the thought of him worrying that he might not be a guy who could interest her... Well... Even though she couldn't help feeling it would have been for his benefit in the long run, she hadn't been able to bring herself to tell the lie. Maybe because she knew what the Bible said about liars. But neither had she been able to bring herself to tell him the real reason it would be better for him to look for a relationship with someone else. And that's where the cowardly part came in. The truth was plain and simple. She didn't want to live without him.

Over the past two years, if she was honest with herself, every guy who'd ever asked her out had been held up and scrutinized in comparison to Jalen. Maybe she hadn't done it consciously, but she'd realized it the moment she'd seen him standing on the soccer field that first day. He was the man she'd been measuring everyone else against.

And they'd all fallen short.

Jalen hiked his slacks up and dropped down to a crouch, peering closely to get a better angle on a play happening on the other side of a cluster of players.

A woman next to Riley spoke. "So you've noticed the new coach too, huh? Isn't he a dream?"

Riley's brows lifted as she turned to see who was

speaking.

The woman had to be in her mid-forties. And her tan was faker than the alligator leather at Walmart. She held a cigarette to her lips and smoke spewed out with her next words. "My boy's on the team, but I have to tell you, I won't mind coming to the games nearly so much this year." She gave a suggestive chuckle.

Riley clamped her teeth together, wondering at the surge of something hot and ugly coursing through her.

A wedding ring on the woman's hand caught her eye as she lifted the death-stick for her next drag.

"Are you married?" The words popped free before Riley could think better of them.

"Oh honey, of course I am. But trust me when I say my Bill hasn't looked that good"—a tip of her head indicated Jalen—"well...ever." Riley's shock must have shown on her face, because beside her the woman laughed. "No need to get all indignant. There's plenty there for all of us to look at."

A gasp from the crowd drew Riley's attention back to the field, and she couldn't say she was sorry to step away from the lady to get a better look at what was happening.

A player from Jalen's team was down but waving everyone off to indicate he was fine. After a moment, he stood slowly and gave the ref a thumbs-up.

"You okay, Charles?" Jalen called.

Charles gave Jalen the same thumbs-up.

"That kid should get a yellow-card!" A father from the stands yelled at the ref. "Come on, ref! You need to protect our kids out there!"

The man was probably Charles's father.

The game seemed to go smoothly for another fifteen minutes with no scores or close shots from either side. Then Remington got open and motioned for the ball from one of his teammates. The boy gave him a perfect pass and Remington beat the one remaining defender between him and the goal.

He's going to score! Riley couldn't deny the excitement building inside her. "Go, Rem!"

Rem was a pace from the top of the goalie box and pulling back his leg to give the shot his all when a defender from the other team slid in from the side and swept the ball away, tackling Rem to the ground in the process. Rem hit so hard that a curtain of water shot up all around him.

"Play on!" the ref yelled.

A huge cry of protest swelled from the home crowd.

Remington was on his feet in seconds flat and Riley could tell by the look on his face and the way his fists were clenched that fury was about to gain the best of him. "Rem!" she tried to get his attention, but he was in the zone and headed right for the ball and the player who had tackled him.

An expectant hush fell like a curtain over the crowd.

Remington blazed toward the guy, and then

dropped into a slide, one leg extended to swipe the ball. The player from the other team went down in a heap and Rem triumphantly passed the ball out to Keith Tuppins at the same moment as the ref's whistle cut a sharp slice across the field.

Rem's hands came up, jaw dropping in a gesture that said, "He got a 'play on' but I get a call?"

But the ref wasn't done. He dug a yellow card out of his pocket and held it up over Rem's head, saying a few words that Riley couldn't make out.

Anger could be read like a book on Rem's face as he stalked away. "Unbelievable!" he yelled.

"Ross, play the game!" Jalen's reprimand was forceful.

Riley glanced over at him. He had his arms folded and one hand cupped his chin. His gaze fastened on her brother in a watchful intensity. But by the way his eyes flickered toward the ref and the dark scowl that covered his face, Riley could tell that Jalen wasn't any happier with the call than Rem was.

That's when Rem's curse rang out across the field.

Disappointment deflated Riley's shoulders. Because she knew without a doubt that Jalen would be a coach who followed his word to the letter.

And sure enough, Jalen snapped his fingers at one of the players on the bench and gestured him toward the center line. Riley couldn't hear what he said over the cheering of the crowd for the play that was happening, but she knew Rem would be sitting the bench for the rest of the game.

She sighed. How many times had she talked to him about his language? Maybe this would be just the lesson he needed to drive her point home.

Now she had to decide... Did she stay in the driving rain to watch a game her brother wouldn't even be playing in?

Like a magnetic power had drawn her, she once again focused on Jalen. Maybe she'd stay to support a different person.

Just the thought seemed to take some of the chill from her bones.

Riley felt deflated when the game ended with the home team losing two to nothing and Jalen having to bench two more of his starters.

Jalen had already told her in a text before the game that he'd be happy to bring Rem home so she didn't have to wait around for him after the game ended. She'd agreed and couldn't deny that she'd done so partly in order to invite Jalen in and spend some time with him this evening.

She'd arrived home, hurried through a warm shower, dressed in a cozy sweater and jeans, and was starting a fire in the living room fireplace, when Remington busted through the door and headed upstairs without saying a word to her. In the doorway, Jalen stood looking a bit miserable with his hands stuffed into the pockets of his slacks.

She couldn't help but smile. "I thought sports were supposed to be fun?"

One corner of his lip did lift. "Yeah, well, trust me, I've had much funner games than this one."

She angled him a sympathetic look. "Want to stay for a bit? Maybe some hot coffee will cheer you up?" She held her breath, hoping he wouldn't turn her down and yet knowing it might be best for the long run if he did.

Something in his expression softened. "Just having you look at me that way is doing the job just fine."

A little fire started in her middle, and when he sank down onto the hearth right next to her, she leapt to her feet. "If you don't mind, finish starting the fire, and I'll grab us that coffee." Before she could ponder too long on what the hint of humor in his expression could be about, she rushed from the room.

He had a cheery blaze going by the time she came back with three mugs on a tray. She'd made up a hot chocolate for Rem, knowing he disliked coffee. She set the tray of mugs on the coffee table and lifted the hot chocolate. "I'm just going to run this up to Rem. Be right back."

Remington was flopped on his bed, still in his rain-soaked uniform, when she tapped on his door and stepped through.

She bit back the reprimand about his wet clothes ruining his perfectly dry bedding and instead offered. "I brought you some hot chocolate."

"Thanks."

She set the cup on his bedside table. "Sorry you had a rough game."

He grunted. "I can't believe he actually pulled me out of the game."

She cocked an eyebrow at him. "He told you all before the game that if he heard you cussing, he would."

Rem sighed. "True. I guess."

She squeezed his toe and then wished she hadn't. *Yuck.* She rubbed the wetness away with her other hand. "You'll feel better if you get a hot shower, Rem."

"Yeah." He levered himself off the bed and took up the mug, heading toward his bathroom. "Hey, Riley?" he stopped on the threshold. "Why do you think Christian people care so much about curse words? I mean, you never used to care until you started going to church and got all religious."

Her heart hammered. *Lord, give me words here.*

"Well, let's just talk about some of the words that are curses." She ticked them off on her fingers. "First, God is the only one who has the power to damn anything, so I suppose the reason most Christian's don't use that is because we recognize it's not up to us. Besides, we're supposed to be a blessing to people and not a curse. Hell, of course, is a terrible place of judgment and is not something to be made light of, so that's probably the reason that word is out. Saying God or Jesus as a curse is using God's name in an unholy, light, frivolous manner, and one of the Ten Commandments speaks against that. And then the Bible tells us to fix our thoughts on things that are true, noble, right, pure, lovely, and honorable. It also tells us not to let any unwholesome talk come out of our mouths, but only what is beneficial for building others up according to their needs. So, I suppose those are some of the reasons that the rest of the curse words"—she jerked a thumb over her shoulder—"are out."

He slurped from his mug with a thoughtful look in his eye. "That might be all good for him, but why does he care what the rest of us do? If we don't believe the Bible, then…" He let a shrug make the rest of his point for him.

Riley felt the question like a zap from a Taser. She pushed down the swell of horror at the thought of her little brother never coming to believe the truths of the Bible. Took a breath. "Well, for one, Jalen is responsible for you guys. Your team represents our school. And the truth is that even people who don't necessarily believe in the Bible will respect you a lot more if you are self-controlled and polite. Plus, Jalen is a Christian and part of what we are called to do is make others think about Truth. His actions certainly have you thinking right? So that's a good thing." She backed out of his room. "Take a shower and then, if you like, come down and we'll make s'mores over the fire."

He grunted his dismissal.

By the time she washed the stinky sock water off

her hands and arrived back down in the living room, Jalen had removed his suit jacket and tie, and had unbuttoned the top two buttons of his shirt and rolled up his shirt sleeves. He sat on the couch and watched her walk across the room, one sinewy arm stretched along the back of the seat.

The temptation to sink right down beside him and curl into his side and let his arm come around her had her wishing for a fan to cool herself. And to think that just a few minutes ago she'd been shivering cold.

She glanced at the loveseat and chair across the room, which in this large formal living room might as well have been in another country.

Jalen followed her gaze and then smirked at her. He patted the seat next to him. "I promise to be as repulsive as possible."

A shiver of something other than coldness whispered through her. "I'll just take this end." She eased onto the far cushion of the couch and reached for her coffee, adding a splash of cream and a teaspoon of sugar.

He let her decision go without any teasing comment. "How's Rem?" he leaned forward to deposit his own mug back onto the tray.

"Oh your cup is empty, let me get you some more." She started to rise.

But he held up a hand. "No don't. I'm good. Really."

She sank back down. "You're sure?"

"Yes." He settled into his corner of the couch

and angled towards her, folding his arms. "How is he?" He motioned with his chin up the stairs.

Riley took a sip. "He's good. You've got him thinking, that's for sure. He was asking me why Christians don't believe in cussing." She smiled.

Jalen shook his head. "I'm sorry I had to follow through on that. Are you okay with it?"

"With you benching him for cussing? Absolutely. More than okay with it."

A little tension seemed to ease from his shoulders. "Some of the parents weren't too happy with me when we lost with three starters on the bench."

Riley sipped from her cup, and then met his gaze as she said, "Well, you made your point. And now hopefully you won't have to again."

"Maybe." He leaned an elbow into the back of the couch and propped his head on one fist, watching her.

She pressed her lips together and wondered what he was thinking behind those gently probing eyes of his. How was it that with one long look the man could fill her with so much peace and so much tension at the same time? She felt like an open book when he looked at her that way and she wasn't sure he would like everything he saw.

She squirmed. "So you are looking for work. Do you want to do the same type of work you've been doing with Justus?"

"I've had my fill of working with troubled kids, I think. Not that every kid doesn't have a few troubles here or there, but working with kids that are delinquent enough to have been to jail a few times is a whole other ball game. I'm glad I had that experience, but I don't think God is calling me to that again. One thing I've thought about a lot is setting up a home for hardworking foster kids who are basically aged out to a point that they likely won't ever be adopted. Ten on up—not many people want to adopt kids that old."

Riley pulled a face.

"I know. It's sad. But there's a real need for kids like that to have a caring place to learn skills and have a safe environment. I could totally get excited about something like that if I had the money to pull it off. Maybe someday with some investors I'd be able to do something like that. For now..." He shrugged. "I'll just take any type of work I can get."

"Like coaching." But even as she said the words, something buzzed to life inside her. Her father's money could totally make that dream come true. But, again, the thought of Dad's money being used for something so pure set her teeth on edge.

You use the money to buy houses.

True, but that was different, somehow. She always repaid the money to the account in full. And it was only the profit that went to the shelters.

Whether Jalen had noticed her wandering thoughts or not she wasn't sure, but when she tuned back in he was saying, "Yeah and I might not have that job for very long if we have too many games like the one tonight."

Riley tilted him a sympathetic look. "It will get better. What do you think you guys need to work on?"

He snorted. "Keeping my starters in the game would help." A small smile tugged at his lips.

"Yeah, but I still think you made the right decision. At this level it's more about teaching them honor and good sportsmanship than anything, don't you think?"

He nodded. "I agree." Then he chuckled. "I just like my philosophy better on the nights when we win. I hate losing." He indicated they should move on to a different topic with the swipe of one hand. "So enough about my miserable evening. How was your day?"

"Good. I think I might have found the next house I'm going to flip and you should see the view! It's here in the Bluffs, just down the street actually. It was the original house that was on the property before it was subdivided and sold off. It was built in the sixties and the owner recently passed away. His kids don't want the house so they are selling it. And it needs a lot of updates. It has all the original fixtures and everything, but I think it has a lot of potential and since the kids just want to get rid of it they are offering it for a song. It just went on the market last night and I put an offer in on it this afternoon before I came to the game."

A small smile softened his eyes. "You really love doing that don't you?"

She shrugged. "Yeah, I guess I do. Seeing an old

place that's all gloomy and run down come to life with a new look and turn homey again...I really do like it."

"You make good money at it?"

She hesitated. Did she tell him that she hadn't taken a penny of profit off of any house she'd ever flipped? Suddenly more than anything she wanted to offer a little piece of her heart to the thoughtful, patient man before her. "Actually, all the profits go to women's shelters. I pick a new one for each house. That's part of the fun."

Jalen reached out and squeezed her knee. "You really are amazing, do you know that?"

She shrugged away the pleasure from his compliment. "It's just a way for me to give back. I don't know where I'd be today if it hadn't been for House of Hope when I needed them. Well, House of Hope and some guy who showed me that Jesus was the only one who could give me all the answers I was looking for." She hoped he could see all the appreciation she was feeling in the look she leveled on him.

He leaned forward and planted his elbows into his knees. "I'm sure if he were here he'd tell you he was thrilled beyond measure when you took him at his word and gave your life to the Lord." He winked.

She sipped her coffee, wishing she could hang on to this feeling of perfect contentment forever.

He angled his head just enough to let her know he was about to lay something heavy on her. "I'm sure he'd also tell you that you should forget what lies behind you and not let your past keep you tied down."

She swallowed, knowing he was speaking about their relationship.

"And I'd have to tell him that sometimes the consequences of our pasts linger on into the future."

He shifted towards her. "Riley, nothing—"

"Someone said something about s'mores?" Rem stepped into the room.

Riley snapped up the excuse to escape from the room. "Yes. I'll run get the stuff. Be right back." She deposited her cup onto the tray and practically ran from the room.

Chapter 12

Jalen watched Riley practically run from the room, feeling somehow like the truth had been snatched out of reach just as his fingers grazed the surface of it.

Rem cleared his throat. "So...ah...Coach?"

Jalen gave him his attention.

"I just wanted to say that I'm going to try and do better."

Jalen wasn't exactly sure if he meant better about losing his temper on the field or better about not cussing, but he sort of hoped he meant both. He nodded. "I appreciate that."

With a puff of relief, Rem sank onto the hearth and pokered the logs closer together.

Jalen resisted a chuckle over his obvious gratification at having the apology, slim though it was, out of the way. He was a good kid. Riley was doing good things for him, despite their messed up parents.

Rubbing his brow, he let his gaze travel over the

expansive ceilings and the expensive, odd, modern-art paintings on the walls, and wondered what it would be like to have so much money but still feel like you didn't have the answers to anything. It must be painful to constantly be searching for that next bit of happiness and never quite finding it. No painting, or multi-million dollar house with a spectacular view, no life-numbing beverage, or beautiful woman could bring the eternal peace people really craved. In many ways it was likely easier for poor people to find the Lord, because rich people always had more money to try out on another fantasy in the hopes that it would be the answer they sought.

Riley padded back in with another tray. Graham crackers, marshmallows, and already unwrapped chocolate bars had been arranged on a plate with artistic perfection.

He was about to tease her about the perfectly arranged tray when the truth hit him square in the gut.

He and Riley came from two totally different backgrounds.

Around his house the s'mores would have been cooked over an open firepit in the back yard. And his mother certainly wouldn't have arranged everything neatly on a platter. She would have tromped out of the house with the box of graham crackers under one arm, and the still-wrapped chocolate bars and bag of marshmallows in her hands. And she wouldn't have let them open a second chocolate bar until the first one was all used up. The marshmallows would have been carefully portioned out, one at a time, along with the crackers.

The headache that had been pestering the back of his skull since the loss of the game flared to life.

Was this what had Riley keeping him at arm's length? And maybe she was right. What did he have to offer her when she came from—his gaze skimmed the inside of the nearly-palatial living room—this? Currently his only income came from his coaching job, and while he had been searching around town for another job he could do, one that came with flexible hours that could give him the days off he needed to travel to away games, he hadn't found anything yet. He did have a small savings account, but it was really only enough for a down payment on a small house if he found that second job. And he had to admit that even though he had degrees in both counseling and social services, no job he might find in one of those fields would keep her in this level of class.

Riley and Remington each wrapped a s'more into a square of tinfoil, then Riley placed them onto the shovel from the fireplace tool set on the hearth and held them out over the coals.

"You like s'mores, Coach?" Rem was practically drooling in anticipation, even as he layered together his next triple-decker s'more.

"I do." Despite his suddenly heavy heart, Jalen smirked at the kid's towering creation. "The key,

I've found, is to build them so that you can actually fit them in your mouth once they melt."

Rem swept a gesture at the stack and offered a cheeky grin. "This is the perfect height. Once it melts, you squish it down and shove the whole thing in!"

"Rem, you better not!" Riley smacked her brother's shoulder with a laugh.

"Watch me." He did rub his hands together this time.

Riley pulled the shovel out and flipped the foil wrapped packets over before holding them back over the fire.

Remington's phone buzzed and when he glanced at it his eyes lit up. He tossed his newly wrapped giant s'more to Riley. "Cook this one for me, would ya? I'll be down for it in a bit." Taking up his phone he headed for the stairs.

One of Riley's slim brows went up. She pulled the shovel from the fireplace and gestured to his first one. "What about this one?"

"Oh, sure, gimme it, right quick." He dashed back for it.

Riley eyed his phone speculatively. "Who you got there?"

The kid's ears turned red just like his sister's were prone to do, and Jalen couldn't help a chuckle.

Remington tried to look peeved. "None of your concern, Ri." But he had a huge grin on his face when he took the stairs three at a time with the s'more in one hand and his phone in the other.

Riley looked at Jalen. "He can't be into girls already, can he?"

Jalen tipped her a 'what do you think?' look.

She moaned a little.

"Eat your chocolate. My mother used to say no woman ever had a problem that chocolate couldn't fix."

Riley rolled her eyes and chuckled. "Isn't that the truth! Here." She held out the shovel to him and he moved to sit next to her at the hearth.

"So is it money, Riley? I know I'm not—" He gritted his teeth. Now why had he gone and blurted that out? Normally he was better at controlling the things that popped out of his mouth, but with her, it was like he just wanted to get to know her so badly and it was driving him a bit crazy not to know what was keeping them apart.

He'd caught her with a mouthful of s'more. But her eyes widened at him.

He waved a hand.

She worked at swallowing, licking the tip of one finger, and finally was able to say, "Is what money?"

He massaged his fingers and palm over one cheek, unable to meet her gaze. "Us, Riley. What has you holding me back?"

"Jalen..." She shook her head and tears pooled in her eyes.

He felt like a jerk. "Riley, I'm sorry. I didn't mean..." He'd take her in his arms, but didn't want her to feel like he was pushing her. Instead he had to be content with shoving his fingers into his armpits to keep himself from offering what she likely wouldn't welcome.

She looked at a loss.

In that moment he made a decision. He needed to let this go before he ruined everything with his need to know.

He reached for a graham cracker and layered it with chocolate and a marshmallow. "You know what? Don't worry about it. Let's just relax and enjoy the evening." His gaze landed on the game system hooked to the TV. "In fact, I challenge you to a video game war. What games have we got?"

For a moment, Riley looked uncertain and then slowly her features relaxed. She leaned back and clasped her fingers around one knee. "Oh, I'm not sure you want to go there. You know I'm a master at Super Smash Brothers."

He grinned and slurped chocolate from his fingers. "Smash, huh? I got dibs on Captain Falcon."

One slim red brow arched. "Fox Marth can take Captain Falcon any day of the week."

"No way."

They settled into the loveseat before the TV and at first Riley stuck staunchly to her arm of the seat. But as they battled, and she leaned into her controller alternately with her tongue stuck between her teeth or humorously screeching at him to stop cheating, she seemed to relax.

They were both laughing when the game came to an end with him beating her by only a couple percentage points. He leaned into the back of the couch and looked over at her. He was surprised to find that they were almost shoulder to shoulder and her blue eyes were shining with happiness.

"Your freckles are back today."

She wrinkled her nose and brushed the bridge with one finger. "My concealer must have worn off."

If he wasn't trying so hard not to push her he would have leaned over and kissed them. "I like them just the way they are. Have I told you lately how beautiful you are?"

Riley how many times have I told you to cover up those freckles when you go out? Dad slapped the newspaper down by his breakfast plate and worked at spreading some jam on his triangles of toast. *Go on back upstairs and fix that before you sit down.*

She cussed at him and plopped into her seat, reaching for the glass of orange juice by her plate. *I'm a senior, Dad. I think I know how to do my makeup the way I want it.*

Dad stood and in one lightening swift move he had her by a handful of her hair.

The juice glass slipped from her hand and shattered on the floor at their feet.

He lifted her out of her seat and shoved her hard toward the door. *Don't sass me, young lady. You are a Ross, not some tramp from the trailer park. Now get upstairs and cover up those blasted freckles! Lucia! Get in here and clean this mess up!*

Riley felt the thumping of her heart against her sternum. Lucia had bustled in as she made her way up to her room. But she hadn't covered up her freckles. Instead, she'd waited until she'd heard her father's car pull from the garage, and then come down and gotten into her own and gone to school.

And this was the second time Jalen had mentioned that he was fond of her freckles. Why had she never known before how much it would mean to her to have someone like her just the way she was?

She'd heard it from Dakota in counseling—the fact that she was perfectly made and exactly the way God had intended for her to turn out—but it had never really registered with her how amazing it would make her feel to meet someone who actually agreed with God on that.

Jalen was so close their shoulders were brushing. She wanted nothing more in that moment than to give in to her selfishness and let him kiss her. She could see the desire in his eyes. All she'd need to do would be to lean a little closer...

As if pulled by some irresistible force, she did just that.

All the oxygen in the room suddenly seemed to disappear, and her palms turned clammy.

This is not fair to him, Riley. Like a lightning bolt, the thought jolted her to her feet. She paced away from him on the pretense of shutting down the game console and putting their controllers away.

Finally, she turned to face him from a safe distance across the room.

He had leaned forward on the couch, propped his elbows on this knees, and clasped his fingers together. There was a world of pain in the gaze he lifted to hers.

Just tell him. Her hands trembled as she stretched a gesture between them. "I want this, Jalen. *Us.* I really do. But I also want to do what's fair to you. And there are some things from my past—consequences that I'm going to have to live with—that wouldn't be fair of me to ask someone else to shoulder."

He kept his silence, but as usual his dark eyes spoke volumes. Understanding. Compassion. Grace. Yet a hint of a question too. And the need for more of an explanation.

She opened her mouth to tell him. But suddenly every thought turned to sludge and she couldn't seem to find the courage to give him the awful truth. She snapped her mouth shut again. Pressed her lips together.

His shoulders seemed to sag. And a slight furrow ticked at his brow. He rubbed it with one finger. "God wants to give you a crown of beauty in place of your ashes, Riley. But the choice of whether to accept that or not, is yours. Just don't stay sitting in the ash pile because you feel that's where God wants you. Because that simply isn't true." He tilted her a look so soft and full of emotion that it nearly robbed the strength from her legs. "Will you do me a favor?"

She could only nod.

"Isaiah. Chapter 61. Will you read that, sometime?"

She took a breath. Offered another nod. But needed some space right now before she gave in to her selfishness, rushed across the room, and threw herself into his arms. "Sorry to shut down the party, but I have to be up bright and early for work. I'd better get some sleep."

He stood slowly, and retrieved his jacket and tie, all the while studying her silently. Finally, he paused by the front door.

She kept several steps back to ensure she remained firmly in control.

Standing with his jacket draped over one shoulder, he tilted her a questioning look. "Come hiking with me on Saturday? Rem can come too."

"Sure." In her hurry to get him out the door, the word popped free before she thought better of it.

He rested his hand on the door knob, and a touch of pleasure tucked into the corners of his eyes. "I'll look forward to it. Bring your freckles." With a wink, he left her standing there.

She flopped into a sprawl on the couch, doing her best to hold back her tears. If only she'd found this man before she had so totally ruined her life.

Chapter 13

It was two days before she rustled up the courage to look at the passage Jalen had asked her to read. The day before she'd just hurried through her morning devotions like normal. But on Thursday morning she woke up half an hour before her alarm clock even went off. She was wide awake, and that never happened.

Okay, God, I get the message.

She rolled over and grabbed her phone off the nightstand and pulled up her Bible app. She tapped on Isaiah. And then on chapter sixty-one. And then she tipped her head back against the headboard and closed her eyes.

Jesus, I've been trying to do the right thing now for a couple years. But maybe I've gotten a few things messed up. So I'm asking You to speak to me through Your Word this morning. Jalen seems to think I need to read this passage, so if that's true, please open my eyes to Truth, and give me the courage to walk forward in it.

With a deep breath, she started to read. And as she did, it was like a soothing balm had just been rubbed all over her spirit.

The verses started out by proclaiming that God wanted to *heal the heartbroken. Announce freedom to all captives. Pardon all prisoners.*

She closed her eyes. *That's exactly how I've been feeling. Imprisoned.* While she knew that Christ had died to forgive her sins, she'd still felt entrapped by them. By the results that would forever be part of her life.

The chapter went on to proclaim that God wanted to *comfort all who mourned.*

Tears pricked the backs of her eyes. She had mourned the loss of the little boy who'd been stripped from the safety of her womb by an angry fist. She'd even mourned the loss of the man who'd caused the injury. But it was for all the little ones she might have had in the future that her anger had risen up and refused release.

Jesus...

The words to the passage were blurry now, but she pressed ahead. She saw the verse Jalen had referred to Tuesday evening. That the Lord wanted to *give her bouquets of roses instead of ashes.* And then the words continued... *Messages of joy instead of news of doom, a praising heart instead of a languid spirit.*

Messages of joy... She remembered her thoughts when she'd spoken to Mom, about how difficult it was to be joyful. Maybe that was because she wasn't letting go of the past and fully accepting all the good God wanted to give her?

She lowered her phone to her lap. Could she begin to live with a praising heart despite what she'd brought on herself? *Jesus, help me to let go of the despair. I want to be joyful, but what good can come out of all my messes?*

The next verse made her catch her breath.

It declared that God wanted to rename her an *Oak of Righteousness, planted by God to display His glory.*

She tipped her head back against the headboard. God wanted to use her to display His glory. She had totally mangled her life. And God had still managed to track her down and change her heart. What better way to show His glory? The contrast of her life before and after? But had she been letting Him do that? She bit her lip. Not really. She'd more been wallowing in her ash heap and feeling sorry for herself.

Oh Jesus, forgive me.

She almost quit reading, feeling too overwhelmed to go on. But after a moment she decided she could always come back to read it again if she couldn't absorb all the Truth with this first reading.

They'll rebuild the old ruins, raise a new city out of the wreckage. They'll start over on the ruined cities, take the rubble left behind and make it new.

A sob tore through her. God could do that for her? God *would* do that for her? She'd certainly made a ruined city, a heap of rubble, out of her life. And for the past two years she'd felt like hope and joy were only for people who hadn't totally messed up the good things God had given them like she had. But now...

Oh how she longed for that fresh start. To simply let go of the past and realize there was nothing she could do about the mistakes she'd made in it. She could only start over from right now and do her best from this point forward.

And God *wanted* that fresh start for her! Wanted to reveal His love to the world through it.

Joy welled up, and now her tears were ones of sheer happiness.

The last two verses had her crying and smiling at the same time as she read them through her blurred vision.

I will sing for joy in God, explode in praise from deep in my soul! He dressed me up in a suit of salvation, he outfitted me in a robe of righteousness, as a bridegroom who puts on a tuxedo and a bride a jeweled tiara. For as the earth bursts with spring wildflowers, and as a garden cascades with blossoms, so the Master, God, brings righteousness into full bloom and puts praise on display before the nations.

Riley leaned forward and got on her knees. She bent over them until her forehead rested on the crumpled blankets. And she sobbed in repentance, in mourning, in joy, and in wonder over the fact that God wanted to bring righteousness into full bloom in her life, to use her life to put praise on display before the nations.

How He was going to do that, she wasn't sure. But she was more than ready to climb off her ash heap and walk away from it.

Jesus, thank you!

She'd never felt lighter as she climbed from her bed and went through her morning routine. Before she headed downstairs to grab a bite to eat, she picked up her phone and texted Jalen. *I read that passage. Meant so much to me. Thank you.*

Chapter 14

Between Jalen's practices, an away game for the team, and her work schedule, Riley wasn't able to catch more than a glimpse of Jalen for the next two days. But they'd shared a series of text messages, and Riley could tell from his tone that Jalen was doing his best to respect the distance she'd put between them. The problem was, now, more than anything, she wanted to zap that distance into oblivion. But she wanted to tell him face to face, not in a text.

She didn't know how God was going to work the future out, but she knew that she was no longer afraid to climb aboard for the ride.

So Saturday morning when Jalen arrived in the driveway to pick them up for the hike, Riley actually ran out the front door, raced across the aggregate, and threw her arms around his neck.

"Whoa!" He took a step back to absorb her weight, but his arms came around her.

His black leather jacket was cool beneath her

cheek in the morning air.

She felt him press his chin into her hair. "To what do I owe this pleasure?" His voice was a low rumble that sent a quake through her.

She eased back, straightened the collar of his jacket, and then smoothed her hands over the front of it. Timidity overtook her and she studied the zipper pull closely. "If you're still willing, and are able to give me some time to figure a few things out, I'd like to give us a shot." She bit her lower lip and peeked up at him.

He dropped his forehead against hers. "You have no idea how happy that makes me, right now."

"Really?"

His sound of agreement was merely a low rumble in his throat.

"Good. Let me run back inside and get Rem." She darted away from him, knowing she might be sending a bit of a mixed message by abandoning him only seconds after such a bold proclamation, but also knowing she needed a few moments of solitude to tamp down the thrill of her new reality.

Half an hour later, Riley stood at the base of the trail and looked up at the steep incline stretching into the trees. She propped her hands on her hips and looked over at Jalen, who was still cinching his backpack into place and retrieving his water bottle from his car. "What are you trying to do? Kill me?"

His lips quirked. "Getting your heart rate pumping is good for you!"

She lifted one brow. "You won't be so smiley when you have to pack me out on your back!"

Remington shoved by her then, stuffing earbuds into his ears, his scowl etched deeply.

Jalen glanced from Rem to her and lifted a questioning gesture. Her brother had been surly and sullen from the moment he'd climbed in the car this morning.

Riley lowered her voice. "He didn't want to come with us, but since I didn't have any place for him to go, I made him come. The lack of computer games for a few hours just might be the death of him." She rolled her eyes, and started up the trail after her brother.

Backpack and canteen in place, Jalen fell into step by her side, and reached over to squeeze one of her hands. "You're a good sister."

She savored the feel of his fingers wrapped around hers. And her heart soaked in the comfort and support Jalen was offering.

Why can't you ever do anything right, Riley?

Riley, almost fourteen, blinked hard to keep her tears back. Dad never liked it when she cried.

She brushed one of her pigtails behind her shoulder, settled on the concrete of the drive next to Rem, and draped one arm around him. The scrape on his knee looked like it hurt and she wished there was something she could do to fix her mistake.

You were asked to watch him for one *afternoon! And this is what happens when you are in charge?* Dad swept a gesture to Rem's knee.

But I was *watching him, Dad. He just turned too sharp on his scooter.*

The slap jolted her head back.

Rem's crying increased.

Don't talk back to me, young lady! Get in the house and get to your room.

When she was slow to respond, Dad leaned toward her once more and she scrambled back in a crab-crawl to do his bidding. But she wished she'd been allowed to stay and help comfort Rem.

"Riley, you okay?"

Riley blinked and looked up. With surprise, she realized she'd come to a stop in the middle of the trail. Jalen had taken a few steps beyond her, but he was still holding her hand and their arms stretched between them.

A quick flip of her wrist waved away his concern, and she used the excuse of starting back up the hill to avoid eye contact. "Sorry. I was just lost in thought there for a minute."

He settled into the space beside her once more. "Care to share?"

She adjusted her backpack. "I was just remembering a time when I was watching Rem and he got hurt. My dad wasn't happy with me."

They strode in silence for a few steps, and then he said. "And looking back at it with adult eyes, was it your fault?"

She tilted her head and thought. "No. I don't think it was."

As usual, he let his silence do the talking for him, but Riley got the message. She shouldn't feel guilt over something that couldn't have been prevented.

After a long moment he squeezed her hand. "I'm sorry you had to go through that."

They were nearing the apex of the hill and Riley did her best not to puff too loudly as she tried to breathe and carry on a conversation at the same time. "Thanks. I was thinking the other day at the trial that I'm not sure if I would ever have come to know the Lord if I hadn't gotten to such a low place in my life. So when I think back, I try to be thankful for the hard times. But after reading that passage in Isaiah the other day, I realized that most of the time I'm probably my own worst critic." She leaned in to the incline. Would he think less of her because of that? She gave him a sideways glance to gauge his reaction to her next words. "Letting go of the critical voices can be a battle sometimes. But I'm hoping to do better in the future."

His fingers tightened around hers. "I'm proud of you, you know that?"

She took a breath. The man likely had no idea how much she reveled in words like those. "Thanks."

They strode in silence for a ways, for which she was thankful because this was the steepest part of the trail. But she could see the crest and hoped there would be a reprieve waiting for her on the other side.

When they topped out on the hill, she noted that Jalen wasn't even breathing hard.

She bent and propped her hands on her knees. "Can I just say it's really not fair that you aren't even a little bit out of breath, right now?"

He grinned and held out the canteen to her. "The view just a ways down the trail will be worth it, I promise."

She gave him a skeptical look over the top of the canteen.

"Don't believe me?" He accepted the water back from her and took a swig himself.

She angled him a look. "Are there going to be any more hills like that one?"

He stepped closer and lowered his voice. "If there are, do you promise to look at me all cute and haughty, just like you are doing right now?"

She propped her hands on her hips. "And if I do?"

He offered her a flash of white teeth and his gaze slipped over her like a warm embrace. "Well, we'll just have to see what happens, won't we?"

A thrill of anticipation stuttered her heart rate

and pebbled her skin with goose flesh.

He tipped his head to indicate the trail. "Shall we?"

Jalen had been right about the view just ahead being worth the hike. They rounded a corner and came out onto a jutting promontory that angled out above the slope of the hill they'd just climbed.

Rem was already seated on a log bench, taking in the view. But Riley was too much in awe to leave her feet.

Below them evergreen trees, aspens, and the occasional stand of madrona trees created a variegated green patchwork that appeared as soft as microfiber. The hill fell way on a steep incline, seemingly right into the aqua waters of the Pacific.

Jalen leaned past her and pointed. "Marinville is right over there."

She followed his finger and found the miniscule cluster of buildings huddled along the coastline. The sun was high overhead now and glinted off the surface of the ocean. Far out she could see a tiny white sail on a fishing vessel, and cirrus clouds hung wispy and fragile along the far horizon.

"Jalen, this is amazing," she breathed.

He stood beside her, hands in the pockets of his cargo shorts, taking in the view with her. "God did good, huh?" After a moment, he tapped her arm with the back of his hand and then thumped Rem on his shoulder. "There's more. Come on."

He led them back into the trees and further down the trail until they crested into a green meadow bordered by a chatty little creek. There was a picnic area and the trees had been carefully weaned so that the view to the ocean was visible and only hindered by the occasional thick gnarled trunk.

Rem plunked himself down at one of the empty tables. They seemed to be the only ones taking advantage of this trail on this crisp fall day and had the park to themselves. Riley was gratified to see that Rem at least took a few minutes to enjoy the scenery before he pulled out his phone, stuffed his earbuds back in, and started playing some game. She glanced over at Jalen and lifted her hands in a what-am-I-to-do gesture.

He smiled and gave her a consoling look before he asked. "Ready to eat?"

"Sure." She settled onto one bench at a table that gave them the best view of the overlook. "Or if there's a better place later on, I'm good with that too."

Jalen strode over and dropped a sandwich and a bag of chips on Rem's table, tapping her brother on his shoulder to make sure he noticed the food. Then Jalen returned and sat down beside her. "I packed tomato soup in a thermos that should still be pretty hot. Or I have ham and cheese sandwiches."

Riley rubbed her chilled hands together. "Tomato soup sounds wonderful."

Jalen pulled out the thermos and filled the lid with the still steaming soup.

"Mmmmm." Riley inhaled the spicy aroma and wrapped both her hands around the warmth of the cup.

Jalen leaned close and bumped her with his shoulder. "I can think of better ways to warm up your hands, just saying." He set one hand on the table and curled his fingers like he was hoping she'd put her hand into his.

With a hint of mischief creeping into her tone she offered. "Gloves? Yes, I really should have remembered to bring some."

He chuckled. "Spoilsport."

She only blew on the surface of her soup. "Care to say grace?"

His grin bloomed larger than life and he waggled his fingers again.

Joy bubbled up from inside Riley in a way she hadn't felt it in a long time. "Okay, you win." She settled her hand into the warmth of his and bowed her head.

As Jalen said grace, thanking God for the food, the beautiful creation, and equally beautiful company, Riley realized she hadn't felt this content in years.

When he'd finished saying the prayer, she found that even though eating one handed was a challenge, she couldn't muster up the willpower to withdraw from his clasp. And so they sat quietly, eating their lunch, and enjoying the view and each other's company. Jalen offered her more soup, but she declined, feeling perfectly satisfied for the moment.

She closed her eyes and tipped her face into the sun, relishing the feel of the rays on her skin, and tuning in to all the sounds surrounding them.

Jalen released her hand to pack up the lunch items and she immediately missed the comfort of his touch. She folded her hands into her lap and rubbed one thumb over the pad of her palm where she could still feel the warmth of him.

Riley woke with a groan. Everything in her hurt. Even her eyes when she opened them to the much too bright lights of a hospital room.

She frowned. What was she doing here?

And then it all came back to her. Nate had come home drunk. Been upset because she'd already put dinner away hours before. She'd tried to leave. Marie, her new friend from Mom's Gym had said she could come by anytime she needed anything. But Nate had caught her.

Riley's hand slipped to her stomach beneath the blankets. Had she really—

A doctor stepped into her room just then. "Hello, Miss Ross. I'm Doctor Clay."

She nodded at him.

"How are you feeling?"

She'd wanted to roll her eyes at him. How did he think she felt when her boyfriend had just held her into the corner of the kitchen cabinets and beat the life out of her? "Everything hurts."

"Yes, well, that doesn't surprise me. I'm very sorry this happened to you." His face turned soft.

Maybe he wasn't so bad. But what was there to say? She didn't reply.

The doctor cleared his throat. "Listen, I'm afraid I have some bad news."

Riley couldn't find the strength to do more than watch him.

"Nate Carlisle was killed in a car accident out on Highway 101 tonight."

Riley blinked. And despite the fact that she ought to feel relief, she could only feel sorrow. But her eyes remained dry.

"There's more. I'm afraid you've lost the baby."

That broke her, and her face crumpled. "Was it a boy like they said?"

"Yes." The doctor cleared his throat and she could tell from his expression that he wasn't done giving her the bad news yet.

She watched silently.

"There was extensive damage to your uterus. The chances of you being able to have children in the future are very slim, Miss Ross."

Riley rubbed at a knot on the picnic table in front of her and watched Jalen rinse the lid of the thermos in the creek.

She had to tell him about her physical

limitations at some point. The problem was, now that she'd decided she wanted a relationship with him, she was a little bit nervous that he might not respond in his predictable easy going and accepting way. What if he broke things off? She forced herself to remember the verses from Isaiah and the fact that God had good plans for her future. Even if they weren't exactly what she might want, she didn't want to climb back on her rubble heap. If Jalen did reject her she would just have to deal with it.

She released a breath through her nose, not certain of anything but the fact that she'd never felt this attracted to anyone before, and that it was only right that he had all the facts before things progressed too much further.

With the lunch items put away, Jalen unzipped an outside pocket of his backpack and pulled out a black rounded leather case that looked like it was for a pair of glasses.

She frowned. She didn't know he wore glasses.

But when he lifted the top, the box did not contain glasses but a sleek silver harmonica.

Jalen pumped his brows at her, and then lifted the instrument to his mouth. A long plaintive note drifted into the afternoon stillness, and then he launched into "Amazing Grace."

Riley quickly realized that Jalen was stunningly good. She swayed gently to the music and simply let herself revel in the view, and the sunshine, and the pleasant bluesy notes.

When he finished that song and dropped his

hands to the table, she clapped softly. "That was beautiful, Jalen. I didn't know you could play like that."

He offered a sheepish smile and twirled the harp through his fingers.

She'd embarrassed him! She grinned and propped her head onto one hand. "Can you play jazz?"

Jalen tapped the instrument against one palm. "I think so. Maybe just a little."

It was the humor ticking up one corner of his mouth that let her know he was being falsely modest. She bumped his shoulder with the back of one hand. "Let's hear it."

What followed was probably the most heartfelt rendition of "What a Wonderful World" Riley had ever heard.

Jalen played a few more songs and then they headed out to finish the loop of their trail.

The rest of the afternoon passed much too quickly and all too soon Riley found herself standing in the entryway at home, preparing to say goodbye to Jalen for the evening.

As soon as they'd pulled into the drive, Remington had leapt from the car, hardly giving it time to stop, and had disappeared up the stairs to his room. He probably already had his headphones on and his Dolby chat going with some friends on one game or another.

The silence of the house wrapped around Riley and Jalen.

Riley tucked her hands behind her back, leaned in to the wall by the door, and kneaded her lower lip with her teeth. "I had a really good time. Thanks for inviting me."

He was holding his sunglasses, and he worked the stems back and forth even as he watched her in that silent searching way of his. "The pleasure was mine." His voice was pitched so low she might not have heard it but for the fact that she was so intently attuned to him right this second.

A thought occurred to her. "There were no more steep hills for me to complain about."

Humor crinkled his eyes, and he took a step nearer. "I guess there weren't. But you could give me that cute haughty look again anyhow, and I could show you what I had in mind for retaliation."

She suddenly felt like all the world had faded away except for the two of them. Her breathing was a bit shallow, and she lifted one foot and propped it against the wall behind her as though she needed the extra grounding.

She couldn't resist falling in with his game. "Was it something like this?" She tried to contort her features into something akin to what she might have looked like once she'd made it to the top of that hill, breathing hard. "Or maybe something like this?" She crossed her eyes and stuck out her tongue like a dead squirrel.

He laughed and stepped right into her personal space and leaned his forearm into the wall beside her head. "Yes, definitely that last look. You have it down perfectly."

Her giggle was breathy as she allowed her gaze to drift to his lips. "And what sort of punishment did you have in mind for my out-of-shape-and-dying-for-oxygen complaints, coach?"

"Hmmm…" He inched closer. "Something harsh and demanding for sure. Might have to test out a couple punishments just to see which one works best." He crooked a finger beneath her chin and his thumb stroked back and forth over her lower lip, but despite his humorous words all humor had faded from his features.

Riley willed him closer. Since she'd been the one to close the gap between them the last time she didn't want to be the one to do it again.

He didn't disappoint her.

And when his lips finally touched hers, she felt like all might have just become right with the world. Her hands wouldn't stay tucked behind her. She slipped her palms up over the taut firmness of his torso until she could clasp them behind his neck. But after a moment even that wasn't enough and she was on her tiptoes and leaning in to him.

One of his arms slipped around her waist and pulled her close. She heard the soft click of his sun glasses hitting the tiles near their feet and then his other hand swept into the hair just behind her ear.

He tasted of the peppermints and M&M's they had eaten in the car on the way home, and his cologne wrapped around her in a tantalizing cloud.

She wanted nothing more than to please him,

but suddenly warning bells were clanging in her head.

He must have heard them at the same time, because with an audible growl that was half groan he jerked away and took two steps back from her. His eyebrows were halfway to his hairline and his chest was heaving. He scrubbed one knuckle across his mouth and still his gaze remained fixed on her.

She was fairly certain she probably looked just as stunned. And suddenly she felt shy. To relieve some of the tension she gave a rapid-fire rendition of the dead squirrel face again.

He laughed and then his face immediately turned serious once more. Slowly, he reapproached her. He settled his hands at her waist and pressed his forehead to hers. "Thanks for giving me one of the best days I've had in a long time, Riley."

Now would be a good time to approach the serious conversation they needed to have. But... It would be a shame to end such a lovely day with such a depressing topic. Since she couldn't come up with any other response, she simply tucked her lower lip between her teeth and nodded.

"I'm going to go now." He dropped a quick kiss against the tip of her nose. "Because staying after you kissed me that way would be offering myself like a chained up goat to the dinosaur of temptation."

She chuckled at his *Jurassic Park* reference and debated whether to tell him she was just as tempted as he was. Her shyness returned full force at the thought of revealing so much of what she was feeling, but if they were going to go into this relationship she wanted to go in with all honesty, so she offered. "I think that is a very wise decision because I would be tempted right there alongside of you."

Reluctantly, slowly, he eased back. "See you tomorrow at church?"

She tucked her hands behind herself once more. "I'll be there."

He bent and scooped up his sunglasses. And it wasn't until he shut the door behind himself that her entire reality came rushing back to her. *Love will snake around to bite you in the end.*

She shook the thought away. *God. I'm choosing not to believe that has to be the case with everyone. I've seen plenty of examples of marriages that remained strong right up to the end. I'm trying to choose to believe the promise that You have a hope and a future for me. And that if Jalen and I choose to stand on Your Word, You will walk with us and help us to stay strong through each step along the way. So to start that out right, I'm going to need Your help to have a difficult conversation with Jalen, Lord.* Her hand rested over her barren womb. *Give me the right words and help me to trust You with the outcome.*

Chapter 15

The next Friday afternoon, Riley worked at a kink in the muscle of her shoulder as she waited in the parking lot for Rem—and his coach—to get done with soccer. Between the team's two away games, her work schedule, and two interviews Jalen had been called to, they'd only had snatches of conversation all week.

She couldn't believe how much she'd missed him.

She'd also spent a good portion of the week signing paperwork and going through the new house in the Bluffs to figure out exactly what she wanted to update in it. The place was the biggest challenge she'd taken on yet, but it was also going to be the most enjoyable project she'd tackled.

This morning Remington had asked her if he could go to the school dance tonight. She'd put him off and told him she would give him an answer when she picked him up from practice.

Now as she sat waiting, she cringed. She'd put

off giving him an answer because she very clearly remembered all her school dances and all the non-dancing activity that had gone on behind the scenes.

But at the same time, there were kids who were there just to have a little fun with their friends. And there was also the fact that she was really hoping to finally get the chance to sit down and have a good talk with Jalen, just the two of them.

Hoping and dreading, if she was honest.

But did she use her need for alone time with a man as an excuse to let her brother attend a questionable activity? Sure and *that* wouldn't leave her with a layer of guilt if Rem fell into some life-altering sin at the dance.

She tucked one fingernail between her teeth. What was she going to tell him? Who knew this guardian thing was going to get so complicated so quickly.

Rem was loping toward her from the soccer field when her phone rang. Still pondering her decision, she clicked her Bluetooth ear bud to answer the call without looking to see who was calling. "Hello?"

"Hey, beautiful."

Warmth curled in the pit of her belly. "Hi, Jalen."

Amazing how two words from the man nearly had her melted into a puddle in the driver's seat. It would be really great to get to see him tonight. Decision made. Rem could go to the dance and if he did something stupid she would just ground him for life.

To Jalen, Riley said, "What's up?"

"I need a favor."

Her brows lifted. What could he need from her? It didn't matter, she supposed. She'd be happy to help him with whatever it was. "Sure. I'm happy to help. What do you need?"

"Has Rem mentioned that there's a school dance tonight?"

A tiny warning that she might not get her alone time with Jalen after all, started to flash at the edges of her conscience. "Yes..."

"Well..." There was a pause and she heard him take a breath before he hurriedly continued, "I've been asked to be a chaperone and I'm supposed to bring someone to help me."

Her heart hammered. So much for the conversation she'd wanted to have. Still, her mind immediately started searching through a mental picture of her closet to see if she had anything appropriate to wear.

Ahead of her Jeep, Remington paused to talk to one of his teammates.

She focused her thoughts back on Jalen. The longer she put off telling him the more he would be hurt when she finally got around to doing so. So if she had to tell him in a room full of blaring music, at a high school dance, so be it. She didn't want to put it off any longer. Of course she would go with him.

Still, she couldn't help teasing, "Maybe I could

go hang out with Taysia for the evening and Kylen could join you as a chaperone. I'm sure he'd do a great job."

Silence emanated from the other end. She wished she could see the look on his face right about now. A little giggle slipped free.

"Ah, your cruelty knows no bounds, madam."

She could hear him breathing into the phone like he might be jogging someplace.

"Well, you never said *who* you wanted to help you. Only that you were supposed to bring someone."

She suddenly realized that Rem and his friend were no longer standing in front of the Jeep but were walking toward another group of boys to her right. Hands tucked beneath her legs, she watched them, but was keenly aware of the man on the other end of her connection.

"Well, in that case, let me be very clear about who I would like to accompany me tonight." Jalen was still breathing rather hard into the phone. "You see there's this beautiful redhead who I've been trying to get to know. Her little brother is on my soccer team and she lives in a house up in the Bluffs. Her eyes are as blue as cornflowers and whenever she looks at me I feel just a little bit tongue-tied and weak-kneed. She has such a compassionate heart that she flips houses and sends all her profits to women's shelters. She recently took in her brother. That's the woman I was hoping to take with me tonight, and I was hoping these would convince her to say yes."

A huge bouquet of red roses mixed with small white lilies and blue lupines appeared in front of her windshield. They appeared so suddenly that she jumped a little and then grinned. She finally understood why Jalen had been breathing so hard.

His whole team whooped and clapped. While they had been drawing her attention off to her right, Jalen had jogged around and snuck up on her from the left and now he peered in at her with a rakish grin.

He lowered his voice "Wow, it's good to see you. It feels like it's been forever." He winked at her through her side window, even though he still spoke to her through his phone. "You wouldn't turn me down in front of my whole team, would you?"

Despite the fact that she couldn't keep a smile off her face, she tilted her head and tapped one finger to her lips as though deep in deliberation.

The team of boys guffawed and slapped each other in hilarity.

Jalen glanced at his team and then grinned at her. "You're killing me here."

She relented and opened her door. Climbing out, she accepted the bouquet, and then very purposefully, she threw her arms around his neck and gave him a hug.

Oh boy. That was a mistake. The man was damp from having just gone through an hour-and-a-half-long practice. Still, the scent of his cologne tantalized her senses and made her want to linger right where she was.

It stayed with her when he set her from him with a grimace and an apology. "Sorry. I promise to shower before the dance tonight."

She chuckled and brought the bouquet to her nose. "Mmmm." She looked up at him and lifted the flowers. "Thank you."

He nodded then propped his hands on his hips. "So is this a yes?"

She laughed. "Yes."

He grinned. "Good. I'll pick you up at six?"

Her eyes widened. That meant she had less than an hour to make it home and get ready. "Okay, see you in a bit." She turned back to her Jeep. "Rem, let's go please."

As she drove up the hill to the house, she couldn't help but marvel over the fact that God had so easily flattened all the walls she'd kept trying to put up between them. She only hoped she hadn't ruined a good thing by waiting too long to give Jalen the full truth. Her hands trembled, but she was determined that tonight was the night.

When they arrived at the school dance just before six thirty, Jalen suddenly realized that this might not have been the best place to bring Riley on a date. The music was so loud it was already hurting his ears before they made it into the gym.

Riley pulled Rem to a stop outside the doors and

gave him a quick hug. "Be good!", she yelled above the noise. "We'll meet you right here at nine o'clock."

Rem grinned and tossed a glance between the two of them. Then yelled back, "Just be sure you two aren't the ones who need a chaperone!" With that and a cheeky wink, he disappeared through the double doors into the gym.

Riley gave Jalen an embarrassed roll of her eyes.

He only chuckled. The kid had audacity and that was for sure.

Riley touched his arm. "Jalen, there's something—"

"—There you are." The high school principal stepped out the door right next to them, already looking a bit frazzled. "Things are already starting to go a little crazy in there." He motioned them through the doors and swirled his hands as though directing them to be everywhere and do everything that needed to be done.

Jalen gave Riley an apologetic look for the interruption, but whatever she'd been about to say would have to wait. With the blaring music, he could barely even hear himself think.

Riley lifted her hands to her ears and leaned close to put her lips right near his ear. Even then she had to yell to be heard. "Am I just getting old? Or is this music really loud?"

Jalen repeated her action and spoke directly into her ear. "We might be deaf by the time we get out of here tonight." She laughed and her hair brushed across his cheek when he pulled back. And that was when he decided that maybe this was exactly the perfect place to bring Riley for a first date. He settled one hand at her back and leaned toward her again. "At least I can use the music as an excuse to stay close to you."

She gave him the cutest self-conscious smile he'd ever seen.

And he had to remind himself that he was really here to work. "Let me run find out where we are supposed to be. I'll be right back."

It turned out they were assigned the area near the punch table, but Jalen was also asked to make the rounds of the school hallways every once in a while to make sure all kids remained in the supervised gym.

After two hours, they'd asked four couples to put a little more space between themselves, confiscated two flasks of undetermined content that had been headed for the punch bowl, and Jalen had shooed two couples back into the gym from the hallways. They only had a few minutes left and they'd hardly said two words to each other all night.

But now Riley smiled at him from where she was dipping the last of the punch out for a couple kids. And if that had been the only interaction he'd had with her all night it would have been worth it.

He allowed his gaze to linger, realizing he hadn't yet told her how beautiful she looked. She was wearing a strapless dress that was somewhere between orange and pink, and he loved the smattering of freckles on each of her shoulders. The dress flared at the waist in a way that made his mouth dry, and had roses of the same color sewn into a see-through material that draped over the top of the skirt. A single strand of pearls hung at her throat. The woman, quite simply, took his breath away.

He suddenly realized that she was gesturing to him. He refocused and lifted his brows in question. She pointed behind him. He turned and saw a dancing couple that needed a tap on the shoulders and maybe a bucket of ice water as well. He sighed. So much for admiring the sight of his date.

He was thankful a few minutes later when the principal called an end to the festivities and gave all the kids ten minutes to clear the building and head off campus. The tear-down went quickly and before he knew it he was driving up the hill toward the Bluffs and the night was coming to an end.

He tuned in to the end of the Manchester United game on his XFM.

"Who's winning?" Remington leaned in from the back seat.

Jalen parked in the driveway. "I don't know. Just listen."

Riley's phone rang. She gave him an apologetic look and said, "I was hoping I could talk to you about something. Do you have a few minutes before you need to leave?"

He would gladly give her hours. "Sure."

He remained where he was while she climbed

out of the car and paced up and down the driveway as she spoke into the phone.

Remington stayed with him in the car, and they listened to the end of the European league game and made small talk about a couple of the calls.

But all the while Jalen couldn't take his eyes off the beautiful woman pacing in the moonlight. When her call ended, she folded her arms and put her back to the rig.

Riley had stepped out of the car because she hadn't wanted Remington to know it was Dad on the phone. Two calls from him in as many weeks. What was the world coming to? She wouldn't put it past him to be calling to tell her he'd changed his mind about taking Rem. Then what would she do? Rem was doing so well and really enjoying soccer and starting to do more things with the youth group. She didn't want him to lose all that.

The phone rang for the fourth time and she pressed answer before it could flip over to voicemail. "Hi Dad."

"Riley, listen. I'm calling because I didn't want you to hear it through the grapevine. I'm leaving Mandy. If she comes around asking for money, don't give her anything. She'll be getting a generous alimony check from me. But she's not taking the divorce well."

Riley squeezed the back of her neck and closed

her eyes. Even though Mandy was the secretary Dad had left Mom for, she could find nothing but sympathy in her heart for the woman. "Dad…" She groped for a comment, but her mind was blank. She had no other words.

Dad chuckled. "You actually sound sorry for her! I thought this would be a bit of good news in your week."

A sigh slipped free. "I would never wish heartache on anyone, Dad."

He grunted. "Well her brand of heartache comes with a four followed by six zeroes. So don't feel too sorry for her. I think she'll bounce back fairly quickly. But she's moaning and complaining still, and I don't want you giving her anything if she comes by."

Papers rustled in the background and Riley could easily imagine he was still at work this late on a Friday night.

Bitterness dripped from his next words. "Just be glad no one else has taken an interest in you, Riley. Broken relationships seem to run in our family. Save yourself the heartache and keep your feelings in check." He blew a loud breath and Riley wondered if he was half drunk. "Not that too many guys are probably knocking down your door, but people know you come from money and men will come around just because of that. Don't give them power over you."

Riley closed her eyes. Swallowed away the pain clawing for release from her chest.

"Anyhow, I have to run. I'll trust you to let your brother know." Dead air indicated he was gone.

Despair threatened to engulf Riley.

Money. Her father thought the only reason any man would be interested in her was because of money.

Dad was losing his second marriage and she could hear the pain and resentment spilling out of him. The need to be better. To be caring. But...always money, money, money. If someone was interested in her, it was only because of money. If he wanted to sever another of his close ties, money absolved him from the guilt. To her father, a check was the answer that righted every wrong. Throw enough dollars at a person and he figured all their problems ought to be solved.

What a self-centered outlook he had. No care for the hearts of people.

She dropped the phone to her side and turned her back to Jalen's rig, just needing a few more minutes to compose herself. She lifted her attention to the smattering of stars overhead. *Jesus, my heart hurts. Will I ever be able to escape this cycle of brokenness and pain?* She'd thought she could let go of the past. And she'd thought that part of doing that might be to allow Jalen into her life.

But maybe she was just being as selfish as her father by making that choice?

Maybe the right thing really was to let Jalen go... Not for the reasons her father gave of protecting her heart, but to protect Jalen's.

He was a good man. And he deserved a whole woman. One who didn't come to him with so much duct tape holding her soul together. And Dad was probably right. Maybe there were some families where *broken* was just part of life. Wouldn't the right thing—the thing God would want from her— be to protect others from having to live with this wearying sorrow?

Her heart felt like it had just tumbled from the top of a mountain and had shattered into tiny pieces.

Chapter 16

Jalen rubbed a hand over his jaw. Something wasn't right with Riley. It was as if all the life had suddenly been drained out of her.

The game came to an end with Manchester United winning one to nothing.

Jalen tapped Rem on the shoulder. "How about we head inside now, huh?"

Without waiting for Rem, Jalen climbed out and stepped around to where he could look Riley in the face.

She offered him a stretch of her lips but he could tell it was a forced smile.

There was obviously something she needed to talk about here, but maybe not in front of her brother. "Take a walk with me on the beach?"

She tilted her head, considered for a moment, and then rubbed both her arms with her hands. "It's freezing out here. How about you come in for hot chocolate and"—her gaze darted to her brother—"give me another chance to beat you at Smash?"

Her voice held unnatural levity.

But she was right. The wind sliced icily tonight. He would rather be someplace alone with her, but he was just thankful she hadn't declined him outright. He thought of the fact that she might not want Rem to know anything was wrong. And maybe the call wasn't something she wanted to discuss at the moment for any number of reasons. Trying to follow her lead, he offered her a grin. "Sure, I'd be happy to grind you into dust on Super Smash again."

She snorted and pulled her house keys from her clutch.

Remington clapped him on the shoulder as they stepped through the entryway. "Just don't let Riley be Captain Falcon, or you're a dead man."

Jalen looked over at her in surprise.

She spread her hands in a what-can-I-say gesture. "You did take my guy the last time." Her eyes were dull and held no glitter of humor.

His concern ratcheted up a notch. "We can both be Captain Falcon."

"No way!" the siblings chimed together.

Jalen tossed a look between them and forced himself to continue this conversation that meant nothing, when all he really wanted to do was find out what was wrong with Riley. "Why not?"

Riley didn't answer but Remington offered a shrug. "It's just a Ross house rule. No two people get to pick the same character while playing Smash."

Riley suddenly seemed to deflate, like she could no longer maintain the pretense. Her expression turned stiff and withdrawn. "Rem, how about you have Jalen look at your algebra for a minute while I make us all some hot cocoa and then you can work on it for a bit tonight."

"Aw, Riley!" Remington's protest could have lifted the roof.

Jalen clapped him on the shoulder. "That's a great idea. Come on, I'll make sure you understand the lesson."

Remington was a bright kid and a quick learner. He really only needed someone to explain the concepts to him in a slightly different way than his teacher apparently was. It only took Jalen five minutes to feel sure that Rem understood the basics of the equation being covered, and would do fine on the assignment.

Jalen left Rem in his room working on his homework, and found Riley standing before the stove in the kitchen. A kettle of water steamed but wasn't quite ready to be poured into the three mugs she'd already scooped cocoa powder into.

"Want to talk about that phone call?"

She shook her head. Waved a hand. "It was my dad, and not really. No." But he heard her sniff, even as she carefully turned her face so he couldn't see it.

He approached her slowly, and saw her stiffen. Her spine was ramrod straight by the time he stopped directly behind her. He didn't want to push her, but at the same time, he wanted her to know she could tell him anything.

Her perfume and bare shoulders lured him. He swallowed and settled his hands on her soft skin, letting his thumbs work into the hard knots of tension in her trapezius muscle. He felt a tremor buzz through her.

He leaned forward and peered at her over her shoulder. "You know I'd never hurt you, right?" He kept his thumbs moving in circles.

She swallowed. Nodded.

Relief eased a breath from him. "It's just that sometimes when we are alone, I feel like you are afraid of me. And I don't want you to ever feel that way around me." The skin just behind her ear begged for a kiss, but he resisted. Now wasn't the right time. Right now what she needed was a friend with a listening ear.

"I'm not afraid of you, Jalen. It's just..." She pulled in a shuddering breath, her attention still fixed on the surface of the water in the pan before her.

"What?" he prodded gently.

She spun toward him and pinned him with a hard look. "I probably should have told you this right away, but...I needed time to think it through. This is one of those ash heaps I might have a harder time climbing off of, you know?"

Jalen clenched his teeth together, determined to be supportive and encouraging no matter what she told him. He'd wondered about this all week from the moment she'd said she had some consequences from her past that wouldn't be fair to ask someone else to live with. The only thing he had been able to come up with was that it probably had something to do with her health. And whatever disease she had, he knew they could walk through it together with God's help.

"You want to have kids someday, Jalen?"

That question threw him. Where was this going? He drew her a few steps away from the flame of the stove, then spread his hands. "Someday."

She shifted her gaze and fiddled with her fingernails, and he could see tears pooling on her lower lids. "Well I can't ever give them to you." Her eyes widened a little and darted his way. "Not that I'm saying I'm the woman you'd want to—"

He had his hands cupping her shoulders in one swift move. He studied the pale wash behind her freckles for a moment, and then pulled her into his chest, wrapped his arms around her, and tucked her head in to his shoulder. "Riley. Is this the consequence you were talking about the other night?"

She nodded and relaxed against him, melding against his chest like perfection. He was so relieved he could hardly think. He'd figured an STD, or maybe cancer from smoking, or even HIV due to a drug habit. But he'd never considered this. This was something he could deal with.

She was shaking now, snuffling softly.

Anger swelled up in him so rapidly he wasn't

expecting it. The fact that someone who was supposed to care about her had hurt her so badly… He ground his teeth, and rocked her gently. He feathered a kiss into her hair and angled a look toward the ceiling. *Give me words, here.*

But for a long while no words would come. And so he offered silence, and the comfort of his arms. He pressed his cheek to her ear, dropped a soft kiss against the hairline at the back of her neck, curled his arms around her, and just prayed. Prayed like he hadn't prayed in a long time. Prayed for her peace. Prayed for their future.

Just when she had finally quieted and he had just about figured out what he wanted to say, she uttered the words that nearly took him to his knees.

"It's my fault, Jay." She fiddled with one of the buttons on the front of his shirt. "I stayed with him and I not only killed my baby, but the potential of any others."

"Riley…" He couldn't stand another minute of not being able to look into her eyes. He set her from him, curved his hands around both sides of her face, and made sure they had good eye contact. "What he did to you was *not* your fault. The man was a"—he jailed a few inappropriate words before they could escape and finally settled on— "monster." He clenched his teeth and reminded himself to breathe so he didn't overwhelm her with his intensity. "And as for you being the woman I'd want." He hoped she could see all the love he was feeling. "Yes. You are exactly that woman. I've waited two years for you. Not just because you are beautiful, which you are, but because you have a compassionate heart that puts others first, and I love that about you. And I love even more that you have been letting God grow His image in you, over the past few years." He settled his palm against the smooth skin of her cheek. Felt her tremble.

She brushed her palms over the front of his suit coat. "I know what that passage in Isaiah said, Jalen. But I confess I'm having a really hard time seeing how God could bring something good out of this. And I don't feel it's fair of me to ask you to commit to me when I can't—"

He touched her chin and made sure he had her full attention. "I'm staying of my own free will." He let his forehead fall gently against hers.

One of her fingers traced back and forth over the dip just below his lower lip. "All week I've been thinking that if you would still have me we could maybe make this work. But my father said—" She brushed the rest of that thought away. "It doesn't matter. What does matter is that...now...I think I have to let you go." Her next words were whispered. "For your own good."

He had the sensation that he was dangling from a cliff and had just lost the last inch of rope in his lifeline. "Talk to me, Ri. I don't understand."

Tears stacked up on her lower lids, magnifying her eyes into big blue pools. "You're so good with babies, Jalen. Kids too—like Rem. You deserve to have your own kids someday."

Relief tugged the air from his lungs. Finally, he felt like he had a foundation under him that he could work from. He thumbed away her tears. Settled a kiss against her forehead. Considered how to respond. How to make her see that she was enough for him all on her own? He eased back and curled his forefinger under her chin. "It's you I love, Riley. Not anything you can give me."

She shuddered. Sighed. Then smiled sadly through her tears. "I knew you were going to say that, Jalen. Then for a while I was afraid you might not say it. But deep down I knew what your reaction was going to be. It's why I kept trying to just distance myself from you. Because I knew you would do the superhero self-sacrifice thing. I'm just not sure I should let you do that to yourself."

He frowned and thought back over their evening. She'd been pretty relaxed and happy until she'd gotten that phone call from her father. "You said your father said something. What did he say?"

The water started boiling and she turned to twist off the gas. She planted her palms against the counter and let them take her weight. "He's divorcing his second wife. Her name is Mandy. She was his secretary when he was married to Mom."

Jalen heard the raw discouragement in her tone. "I'm sorry."

She peered over at him from eyes that were dulled by way too much living and hurting for a woman her age. "I know there are relationships that work, Jalen. I've seen them in Kylen and Taysia,

Reece and Marie, and Justus and Dakota. I can't imagine any of them ever falling apart. But there was something else my dad said about relationships in our family being destined to break, and I wonder if he is right? Maybe there are some relationships that are...I don't know...written in the sand before they even begin? And if that's the case why start? If ever there was a woman who was destined to have a relationship that could be wiped out by one wash of a wave, I think I might be her. There's already so much stacked against us. I've done so much wrong. And there are so many reasons why I don't want to hurt you. Why you deserve better."

Jalen's heart was hammering so hard he could almost hear the beat of it in his ears. Because he suddenly knew that she cared very deeply for him and the realization made him the happiest man in the world. He took her hand and tugged her toward the kitchen table. "Forget the hot cocoa for a minute. Come sit."

He eased her into a chair, but had too much energy to sit himself. He squatted in front of her instead. He tapped a fist to his mouth, willing God to supply him with truth and wisdom to pass on to her.

She sighed. "Jalen, I'm trying really hard not to do the selfish thing here. Please don't make this harder than it has to be. You need to let me go. There's another woman out there somewhere who will make you so happy and so thankful we did the right thing tonight."

Her words sliced into his heart, but not because she was trying to push him away. They sliced because she'd been doing so well this week, and then with one phone call, her father had stripped from her the newfound truth she'd been living in. The truth about how special and perfect she was. How God had good plans for her future. How she needed to forget what was behind and press on toward what was ahead, and trust God to miraculously transform the ashes into roses.

But in the face of her resurrected doubts how did he begin to remind her?

God?

And in that moment a breath of truth washed through him and he knew exactly where to start.

"Riley, we aren't acceptable to God, or to others for that matter, because we've lived a perfect life and never made any mistakes."

She pinched at the gauzy material of her skirt. "I know that."

"Do you?" He scooted closer to her, pressed his palm to hers, hooked their thumbs together, and then rested the back of her hand against his cheek. He peered intently into her face, willing her to truly hear his next words. "The only way God accepts us is when we yield and admit that we fall short."

A dry chuckle, brittle and hard, escaped her. "Oh trust me, I know I fall short."

He placed a quick kiss on the back of her hand and then returned his focus to her face. "And that's where the problem comes in, Riley. Because we can't stop there. Once we recognize that we fall short in ourselves, and accept that only the blood of Jesus can cover our sins—which I know you have done—it is *then* that we are made perfect in God's sight. Because of Jesus' blood, God no longer sees our failings when He looks at us. Just a clean slate. Perfectly created in His image."

She tilted him a look full of pain. "I believe that Jalen. But there are still consequences I have to live with because of my past sins. And it wouldn't be fair of me to ask you to live with them too."

"But you aren't asking me. I'm offering myself. Would you deny me the pleasure of that sacrifice because you are afraid of what the future holds?"

Her eyes widened, and he knew then that he'd hit on exactly what the issue was. She knew he cared for her now, but she feared that her deficiencies would drive them apart in the future. She'd had a lifetime of people drilling into her that she wasn't good enough the way she was. And all he wanted was the rest of her lifetime to drill into her that she was perfectly amazing, just the way she was.

"Do you know Jeremiah 29:11?"

She pursed her lips, but nodded.

"God knows the plans He has for you, Ri. Plans to prosper you and not to harm you. Plans to give you a hope and a future." He squeezed her hand. "It doesn't say that promise is only for people who've somehow managed to live their lives in a way that hasn't resulted in a lot of painful or lasting consequences. It's a promise for everyone."

He stood and pulled her with him. Purposely, he invaded her space, wrapping one arm around her waist and pulling her close. "I want to be part of that hope and that future, if you'll have me."

A shudder coursed through her, and the tears that had been lingering just below her lashes, rose and spilled over. "I'm sorry, Jalen. But I just can't." She pressed him firmly away and strode the few steps to the stove, keeping her back to him. "Please. Don't make this harder for me than it already is. I want you to leave."

Defeat drained any last arguments from him. For a long moment, he remained where he was, willing her to turn and say she hadn't meant it.

But she remained resolutely stiff and stolid.

Jalen rubbed at the pain in his heart. Empty. Lifeless. A desert wasteland filled with nothing but dry bones. That was what he felt like.

Slowly, he made his way past her. Through the formal dining room, the entry, and the front door. The wind caught the heavy wooden door and it crashed shut behind him with a slam. Like the final stroke of a judge's gavel in the sentence of his life.

Chapter 17

The next weeks turned into a depressing routine for Jalen. The warm colors of fall were fading to the gray colors of winter. He'd taken a job as the groundskeeper for Serenity Shores and really hoped that Reece hadn't created the job just to give him some employment.

He enjoyed the work. It was backbreaking, and the grounds could pretty much sponge up all the time as he wanted to invest in them—which was basically every spare minute he had outside of his coaching and game day responsibilities—to keep his mind occupied and off of Riley.

His team was doing well and he was proud of his boys. They'd made the playoffs and had the first game of the bracket next Saturday.

Right now he was working to organize the groundskeeper's shed at Serenity Shores. A few of the rental cabins had fireplaces, and before Reece's father had passed away he'd just started dumping the wood behind the shed and covering it with a tarp. But some of it still rotted that way and Reece hadn't had the time to do anything about it since he'd taken over after his father's death. So Jalen had reorganized the interior of the shed and cleared space along one wall. He was in the process of chopping the wood and stacking it into neat rows.

He let the ax bite deep into the chopping block and then gathered up the armful of logs he'd just split. Sweat dripped into one eye and he relished the sting of it.

What would Riley be up to on this chilly Friday afternoon?

He grunted, elbowed through the door the wind had blown slightly shut, and dropped his armload onto the second row of blocks he'd started stacking. The first row stretched the length of the shed and rose to the level of his head.

He'd thought giving Riley some time would maybe bring her around. But his hopes had been dashed as night after night he'd fallen into his sheets with exhaustion clinging to him and the knowledge that he'd just spent another day without even a hint of a heart-change from her.

He swiped a wrist across his forehead and turned to head back out for another armload.

Reece stood outlined in the light spilling through the doorway, pulling on a pair of work gloves.

Jalen paused.

Reece remained blocking the way, taking in the changes to the interior of the shed.

Jalen almost hoped he wouldn't be happy with it. That would give him the excuse to redo it all over again. Mind-numbing work.

But Reece only nodded in satisfaction. "Looks good." He lifted one gloved hand. "I have a few minutes to help. Marie has the day off today so she is taking care of the front desk."

Jalen clenched his teeth, wishing he could find an excuse to go work on another project that would allow him to keep his solitude. The problem was, there wasn't a thing he could think of that needed doing around the place right now, and Reece would see right through his ploy.

Reece stepped outside and set a round up on the chopping block, lifting the ax high and severing the wood in three swift blows.

Jalen lifted one of the split halves and set it on the block, stepping back so Reece could take his swing.

"You're putting in a lot more time around here than I'm paying you for, Jalen." Reece let the ax fall with a grunt.

Jalen watched Reece split the log into several smaller segments before he offered a shrug. "I don't mind. I'm happy for the work. And it all needs doing."

Reece held his silence as they worked together to chop through several more rounds of wood. But finally he paused, propped the head of the ax against the chopping block, and his arm against the end of the handle. He pulled a bandanna out of his back pocket and pushed his cowboy hat back on his head to wipe his forehead. "So, you just going to let her push you away like that without a fight?"

Jalen clenched his teeth, gathered an armload, and tromped into the shed. He might have known Reece had ulterior motives in coming out here to work with him.

When he tried to leave the shed, Reece met him at the doorway, blocking his way with his arms full of wood. And Jalen could see the man had no intention of moving until he got some sort of an answer.

He sighed. "Just drop it man. I gave it my best shot. And she doesn't want me. So... what's a guy to do?" He stepped out of the way and motioned Reece past him.

Jalen left him there, took up the ax and set up another round on the block. This time he'd be doing the chopping. He needed to work out some of his anger.

Jalen hadn't made it through but half a block when Reece reappeared, and it was obvious he had no intention of leaving.

Jalen made quick work of several rounds, lifting the ax high and swinging it hard. Each time the blade connected with wood the vibration jolted through him, pinching at muscles that burned with the effort.

Reece propped his hands on his hips. "So you're perfectly happy to get on with your life without her then? Because if so I'll just keep my mouth shut."

Jalen glowered at him. Reece knew the answer to that question before he'd even asked it. Of course he wasn't happy to move on without her. The problem was he'd already played all his cards and she'd rejected each and every one. He didn't have any moves left.

Jalen gulped for air as Reece set up another block for him, taking his sweet time about getting out of the way.

Reece twisted the block around, slowly aligning a slight crack so that it would match a parallel line with Jalen's blade. "Talk to me, man. You might as well talk to somebody. It's been weeks and you've yet to tell anybody, that I know of, what even happened. All of us thought things were going well for you two and then...they weren't."

Jalen swiped his forehead against the sleeve of his shirt and stared down the hill to the pulsing ocean beyond. Where did he even start? "I don't know, man. I think she's afraid of the future. She said..." He searched his memory for her exact words. "She said, some relationships are written in the sand before they even begin and that one wave can wipe them out. And that she felt like I needed a better woman than her." His voice broke on those last words. Nothing could be further from the truth, but he didn't know how to make her see the truth of it. "I tried to tell her... But..." He shook his head and gritted his teeth against the tears that wanted to spill and the break in his voice that wouldn't even let him complete a full thought.

Slowly, Reece took the ax from him and leaned it against the chopping block. "I'm sorry, man. I know God can help you both work through this because just a couple years ago Marie and I were both right where you two are at now." Reece clapped him on the shoulder. "I'm praying for you, and for her. God can help you figure out a way to show her that with Him as your foundation, life's waves might crash over you, but they can't shake you."

Jalen kicked his toe against the bark of the chopping block. While he was glad for Reece that things had worked out for him and Marie, he wasn't naïve enough to think happy endings came about for everybody. Still, he tried to offer a smile. "Thanks. I appreciate it." He socked Reece in the arm. "Now quit pretending you are out here to work with me and go enjoy your wife's day off with her. I've got this."

Reece chuckled, pulled off his gloves, and sauntered down the hill toward the house, but he paused a few steps away and turned to pin Jalen with a look. "Are you just going to walk away then and let her believe she's been right all along and that love can't last?"

Jalen chucked a piece of wood at Reece.

Reece dodged it and gave him a friendly glower. "That's no way to treat your boss!"

As Reece headed down the hill, Jalen went back to work on the wood, but as he did so he couldn't shake Reece's words from his mind.

With Him as your foundation, life's waves might crash over you, but they can't shake you.

An idea was forming.

Riley pulled her Jeep to a stop in the parking lot of Victoria's Tea and Crumpets and clenched her keys into her palm. She gave herself a stern look in the rearview mirror. "You can do this."

Taysia, Marie, and Dakota, who'd been back from her honeymoon in Cancun for a couple weeks now, had cornered her in the foyer on Sunday and insisted that they all go out for tea and a movie today. This was normally a little restaurant that she loved coming to, but today she knew her friends had ulterior motives.

She'd seen the sorrowful pitying looks they each had cast Jalen's way when he passed them in the church entry.

Riley would rather be just about anywhere else—she'd even contemplated setting up a dental appointment—but if she and Jalen were going to get on with their lives and live in the same town as each other, neither of them could avoid the tension on this front side of their breakup. Eventually everyone would get the picture and realize they weren't together. In fact, if they didn't live in such a nosy, gossipy, tiny town to begin with, no one would likely have even known they were together in the first place.

She climbed out and stuffed her keys into her purse as she pushed through the windowed door. The lace curtain wafted a little on the breeze she created as she entered. Several wrought iron shelves right in the entryway displayed tea sets and beautifully canned preserves that were for sale. Glass canisters of tea leaves along the shelf to her right, each with a little silver scoop inside, boasted such names as Ceylon, Darjeeling, and Malawi. She made a mental note to buy several ounces of the Malawi tea before she left today. It had been her favorite tea since the first time she tasted it.

Victoria, the elderly lady that owned the shop, stood behind the register and peered at her over her bifocals. "Hello, dear. Go on back to your regular table. The girls are all here already."

Riley forced a smile and headed toward the little back room where they had all gathered once a month for the past couple years. This should be normal. Routine. But she couldn't help feeling like a student taking the dreaded walk to the principal's office.

Just as she'd feared, while the girls all smiled and tried to chat amiably, there was a stiff atmosphere around the table as they ordered and ate. Riley ate in silence, just waiting for the hammer to drop and praying they would be understanding about her reasons for needing to walk away from Jalen. Because if she didn't have the support of her best friends, she didn't think she could keep on breathing—that was already hard enough without

Jalen in her life.

Just as she'd suspected, once their plates were cleared, all three women fixed their gazes on her. She could practically feel them leaning over her like aggravated school teachers over a wayward pupil.

She held up a hand to ward them off. "I know why we're all here today, and I have something to say in my defense."

Taysia's brows went up, and Riley could have sworn one corner of her mouth had started to lift with humor before she suppressed it.

Marie twirled her small silver spoon through the tea in her cup, a world of understanding softening her blue eyes.

And Dakota, who knew Jalen the best out of the three of them because of how closely he'd worked with Justus, didn't even try to disguise her disgust. She folded her arms and huffed, "This ought to be good."

Taysia reached over and laid a hand on Dakota's shoulder. Which did silence any further words from her, but didn't remove the glitter of ire from her gaze.

Riley swallowed away her trepidation and forged ahead. "I know each of you like Jalen and would have been pleased to see us get together. Trust me when I say I haven't missed any of your pointed remarks over the years about what a great catch he would be for some lucky woman. But all of you know my history." She pleaded with Dakota with her eyes. "Dakota, you of all people know how broken I was when I came to House of Hope. I'm like a vase that got shoved out a third story window, and yes, now I'm mostly glued back together, and God has done some amazing stuff in my life, but there are still cracks and scars and chips missing in places. You know my...limitations. And..." Drat! She'd told herself she wasn't going to cry. But the tears welled up despite her resolve and blurred her vision. "I'll be the first to admit that Jalen really is a wonderful guy. Any woman would be blessed to be with him. And I wish..." She cleared away the blockage that seemed to have stopped up the words in her throat. "I wish it could be me. But it would be selfish of me to let him settle for me. Even though that's what he thinks he wants right now."

The three women seemed baffled and looked back and forth between each other as if they couldn't come up with a response.

The first hint of ease since she'd walked through the door whispered through Riley. She'd known that if she could just state her case they would come around to seeing it her way.

Finally, Dakota opened her mouth, about to speak, but Marie snapped one finger into the air and waggled it sideways at her. "I've got this."

Riley blinked, a little taken aback by the anger she saw shimmering in Marie's normally placid blue eyes.

Marie leaned towards her. "Riley Ross that is the stupidest excuse I've ever heard in my life."

Taysia took an audible breath and cleared her

throat.

Marie blinked, eased back a little, and smoothed a hand over the tablecloth. "Okay, so maybe that was a little harsh. Sorry. But I can say that in all honesty because that is pretty much the same excuse I used with Reece and I want you to know that I totally understand your fear."

Riley blinked. "Fear?"

"Fear of loving and letting yourself be loved. Fear that you'll mess something up in the future and all the good things God has brought into your life will suddenly come crashing down around you like they always have in the past."

Riley toyed with the demitasse spoon on her saucer. She felt the pinch of her brow. "If I'm honest that might be part of my reasoning, yes. My dad said something to me about all Ross relationships being destined to be broken and that's when I realized that I might be consigning Jalen to a relationship that was doomed before it ever got started."

Marie started to speak, but Taysia leaned forward this time with her finger up, indicating it was her turn. "You're approaching love with the wrong attitude, when you think of it that way, Riley. Love isn't a fluffy emotion that only lasts as long as the good vibes do. Real, lasting and true love is a choice. It's a commitment that you are going to stick with someone through feast or famine. Through messed up family, and sloppy baby kisses. And"—she held up a hand to cut off Riley's attempt to remind her that she couldn't even give Jalen any babies—"even though you can't have kids of your own, God can use that to make you a blessing in the life of a kid who might not otherwise ever have a loving mom and dad." She leaned close as though willing Riley to truly hear her next words. "Will you make mistakes? Of course you will. Will he make mistakes? Of course he will. But with God's help and strength you'll go back to your commitment, your choice, your love, and start afresh. When you build a relationship on the foundation of God's principles it will be lasting."

"Riley Ross…" Dakota leaned forward from her place across the table and speared Riley with a look so full of love, Riley couldn't help but know she cared. "You just remember that you are an amazing woman and you *deserve* a wonderful guy like Jalen in your life."

"So you guys don't think it is selfish of me to want a relationship with him?"

"No!" All three chorused at once.

They each chuckled then, leaving Riley feeling a bit befuddled.

"You know what I think?" Marie squeezed her shoulder. "I think Jalen is a blessing that God wants to bring into your life."

Riley felt her face blanch. And her eyes dropped closed. Jalen was the beauty God had wanted to exchange for the ashes of her past. And she'd practically snubbed her nose at the magnificent gift and hurt a wonderful man in the process.

She winced. "Well even if that was true, it's probably too late now."

A look that Riley wasn't sure she understood passed between her three friends.

"Oh, I wouldn't be so sure about that," Dakota said. "But for now, how about that movie?"

"First!" Marie held up one hand to stop everyone who'd started to rise from the table. "I have some news."

Everyone sank back into their seats.

Marie's face bloomed into the hugest grin, and then suddenly her face contorted. "Riley I'm sorry. I'm an idiot. One of these days I'll learn to think things through before I go popping off at the mouth."

Riley glanced first at Taysia and then at Dakota and it was immediately apparent that neither of them had any idea what Marie was prattling about any more than she did. "I don't understand Marie. What is it?"

Marie looked uncertainly at Taysia. "I was just so excited. I didn't think..."

Taysia tilted her a spit-it-out look.

Marie glanced uncertainly at Riley. "Reece and I...we're expecting."

Joy bubbled up in Riley and bloomed into a grin. She leapt to her feet and yanked Marie out of her chair, wrapping her in a huge jubilant bear hug. "I couldn't be happier for you." She set Marie back from her and looked her right in the eyes to make sure she could see the truth of it. "Honestly." Riley squeezed Marie's shoulders with her fingers. "When are you due?"

"Late March."

Taysia and Dakota were grinning too, and both had tears sparkling in their eyes as they each jostled for a turn to give Marie a hug.

"Guys. We're going to be late for the movie." Taysia shooed them all towards the register out front. "Marie can give us the details on the way."

And as Riley followed her friends and paid for her food and the extra packet of tea, she couldn't help but be abundantly thankful that God had given her such good friends, even if they were a little too happy to tell her things exactly like they were.

Jesus. She closed her eyes as she waited off to one side for Marie, who couldn't seem to stop chattering in her excitement, to pay for her meal. *I think I really messed things up royally this time, but I'm pretty sure You know that already. So…if it's not too late. Maybe You could give me one more chance? This time I promise to not only hear the Truth that You want to bring good things into my life, but to step out and accept the good gift, the good man, when he shows up.*

Chapter 18

Jalen pulled into the driveway of Riley and Remington's house and climbed from the car. His hands were so sweaty that he rubbed them against his jeans. He'd gone for casual and now he was second guessing that decision. Maybe he should have dressed up, but he was here now and if he drove away he wasn't sure he'd ever get up the courage to come flop his heart out in front of her again.

He reached into the backseat and pulled out the bouquet of beach grass and hot pink wild peas. He wasn't sure about that either. It did so little to actually convey the river of emotions flowing through him.

Okay, God. I've done my part to set everything up. Now I just need You to show up and be convincing on my behalf.

Taking in a breath, he firmly pressed the doorbell. He heard it chime deep inside the house and tried not to fidget on the doorstep.

A moment later, Remington opened the door. He stilled. Glanced from the bouquet in Jalen's hands to his face, and then grinned. "It's about time you showed up. She's been mooning about like a sick cow for weeks."

Jalen's heart rate kicked up at the hope contained in those words.

But Remington didn't step back and invite him inside.

He leveled a look at the kid. "So, can I come in? Or what?"

Rem shook his head. "I don't think she'd want you to come in."

Jalen felt his hopes deflate. "I see."

"Because she's not here right now." Remington grinned like he'd just played the best trick of the century.

Jalen narrowed his eyes on the kid, but couldn't help the smile that leaked around his glower. "You're getting set to be assigned a multitude of double ladders at the next practice."

Remington laughed and lifted his hands in an I-surrender pose. "She's down at the new house she's flipping. Just over on Seagull Lane." He pointed in the general direction but Jalen was already heading back to his car.

"I know where it is. Thanks."

Remington leaned far out of the doorway and hollered, "If I pray for her to be nice to you does that get me out of the double ladder sprints?"

Jalen grinned at him over the top of his car as he

laid the bouquet back into the rear seat. "Depends on if your prayers work or not!"

"Hey! That's not fair! All I can do is ask! I don't got the power to make it happen, you know."

Jalen sank into the driver's seat and started the engine, muttering to himself, "Ask away, kid. Because I could really use all the help I can get, about now."

Standing in the living room of the old house gripping her hammer, Riley settled her hands on her hips and surveyed the mound of sheetrock and studding she'd just ripped out. She pulled in a breath through her dust mask.

Taking out this wall was a huge task, but it would be worth it once she got everything finished. It had been strange, anyhow, to have a guest bedroom be the first thing anyone saw when they entered the house. Now the living room would be half again as big and have more lighting due to the extra window.

She skimmed the room in satisfaction. This place had personality, with its double bay windows overlooking the Pacific far below, and the sunburst pediment above the main door's crosshead. Decorative archways also added extra aesthetic touches to several rooms of the house.

If she took long enough to remodel it, she could actually see herself maybe living in this one after she renovated it. Since her talk with the girls at the tea shop, she'd been doing a lot of praying and reading her Bible. And she'd come to realize that her refusal to use any of the money her father had gifted to her might look unselfish on its surface, but was really just a variation of rebellion. She hadn't wanted her father's money to feel like a blessing in her life. And she'd enjoyed knowing that it was just sitting there doing nothing, when in fact she wouldn't have been able to buy or flip even one of the houses without it. She'd been using the money all along to do good things, but instead of recognizing that and being thankful for the blessing of it, she'd only been seeing the bitter reminder of where it had come from. And maybe finally using some of it to do something just for herself would help her be more thankful that she had a father who'd at least provided for her, even though he could have handled the giving of it in a much more mature and kindly manner.

Riley Ross, you have cussed me for the last time, young lady! Dylan stepped into her room and threw a suitcase against her chest.

She caught it on reflex, her eyes widening. What was he up to now? Maybe she shouldn't have cussed him for missing Rem's graduation from third grade. But the disappointment in her little brother's eyes had almost been more than she could bear. And when she'd arrived home to find Dylan sitting at the dining room table sipping coffee and reading the paper, her anger had simply exploded.

Pack yourself a bag. You are leaving here within the hour and you aren't coming back.

The shock of those words crashed over her, nearly taking her to her knees, but her anger held her in good stead. *Whatever, Dylan. It's not like I love living here with your nurturing encouragement and support, anyhow.*

She'd counted herself lucky that he hadn't slapped her for that statement. But she'd seen the hunger to do so in his eyes before he stormed from her room.

He'd given her the stated sixty minutes to pack, and then he'd driven her to town and dropped her off in front of the bus depot. He'd handed her a business card from a bank when she got out of the car, a glint of something hard in his gaze. *User name and password is written on the back. For heaven's sake don't lose this, Riley. There's more than enough in there to set you up in fine style if you work hard and invest it like I've taught you.*

The glare of sunlight through the window brought Riley back to the present.

That was the night she'd gone to Nate's and moved in with him. It had been two weeks before she'd even looked at the bank account and she'd nearly fallen out of her chair after counting the number of zeros behind that three. Her father had set up an account for her with *three million* dollars in it!

She'd never told Nate about the money. Something had held her back, and in the years that followed she was so thankful for that fact.

The money was all still in the same account. She'd changed the account password but still had the card with Dad's scrawl on it tucked into her wallet. She'd thought about throwing it away several times, but somehow could never bring herself to do so.

And now, for the past few weeks, the Lord had been impressing on her to let her bitterness go. That maybe it was time to do a little more with her "talents" than she had been. *What* she wasn't exactly sure yet.

Well okay, there was the one man who'd said he'd love to build a home for above-prime-adoption-age foster kids if he had the money to do it.

Riley's heart thumped at just the thought of Jalen.

Could she get up her courage to go tell him she had all the money he'd probably ever need to pull off his dream project? That she'd be happy to fund it for him? That she was ever so sorry she'd let one stupid conversation with her father make her forget everything God had been trying to teach her lately and that she'd love another chance to climb off her ash heap if he was willing to give it to her?

She let loose a huge sigh.

It had been two weeks since the evening she'd gone out for tea with the girls. Every day she'd prayed and asked God to give her another chance. And every night she'd fallen into her bed after another twenty-four hours of denial.

She needed to start facing the fact that Jalen wasn't going to come to her. Hadn't he proved his patience and willingness to wait during the year and a half that she'd basically cut off all communication with him? If she wanted to see if he was willing to give her another chance, she was going to have to swallow her pride and go to him.

And what's wrong with now?

Her heart rate spiked at just the thought. She glanced down over herself. Her yellow sleeveless blouse and jeans were not her best make-a-good-impression clothes, but she could swing by the house and change.

She pulled her phone from her pocket and checked the time. This late on a Saturday afternoon he should be done with his work at Serenity Shores. Where would she find him?

She suddenly didn't care where he was, she just knew she had to go and talk to him right now. After she changed, if she couldn't get Jalen to answer a call, she would call Reece and see if he knew where Jalen was.

Snatching up her purse and digging out her keys, she transferred her phone to the pocket of her purse, and tugged the door shut behind her. She locked it, spun toward her Jeep, and froze.

Jalen was walking towards her up the walk carrying a bouquet of wild peas and beach grass. He stopped when he saw her.

Today he was wearing a white t-shirt tucked into a pair of jeans, with a blue and white plaid over-shirt left unbuttoned. He apparently hadn't shaved for a few days because there was a thick coating of dark stubble along his jaw and lip. And, *wow*, did she like the look of it.

Her mouth was dry and each breath she took was rapid and shallow.

Despite how good he looked, it was his eyes that captured and held her attention. Today they were such a deep brown they were almost black.

"I was just coming to find you," she blurted.

He tilted his head and studied her in that oh so patient silent way of his.

Did he believe her? She suddenly wanted more than anything for him to know it was true. "I really was."

The corners of his eyes crinkled just a little. "I believe you." He held the bouquet out toward her. "I was bringing you these." His free hand rose to grip the back of his neck. "And hoping we could talk for a bit?" Vulnerability cloaked his features.

She stepped close and accepted the flowers. "They're beautiful. Thank you." She buried her nose in the blooms, but all she could smell was the tantalizing scent of his spice and leather cologne.

Thumbs hooked into the pockets of his jeans, his attention remained on her face. "It's really good to see you."

She questioned him with her eyes. Did he mean that? Hope started to thump out a rhythm in her chest. Maybe this was the second chance she'd been begging God to give her for weeks.

"Would you—" He cleared his throat. Looked down. Kicked at something in the walk beneath his feet. Then looked up and captured her with his eyes again. "I was wondering if you would come to the beach with me? I have something I'd like to show you."

Unable to form any words, she only nodded.

Everything in him seemed to relax. He tipped his head. "It's just to your beach, actually. The one right below your house. Want to drive to your place and walk down from there?"

"Actually the trail from this house leads to that same beach. We could just walk from here."

He glanced at the time on his phone. "Tide's not due in for a bit, so that should work."

Curiosity piqued, she tipped him a quizzical look. "The tide?"

He only folded his arms over his chest and leaned in to his heels. "You'll see."

She lifted the bouquet. "I'll just take a second to put these in water. Come on through. It's a mess in here but we can go out the back to the trail."

He followed her inside and quietly took in the old kitchen while she dug out a plastic cup from her stash and propped the bouquet into the corner of the sink where it wouldn't tip over. She would give them a proper vase when she got them home.

"I'm ready." She rubbed her damp hands nervously against her jeans.

He looked over at her. "This kitchen doesn't look like it's been touched since the house was built."

"I know." She led the way through the grand dining room and into the living room. "It's going to be a blast to fix up." She slid open the slider and stepped out ahead of him. "The old cabinets get torn out on Monday and I already have my eye on this great set of stainless steel appliances. I think I'm going to go with cherry-wood cabinets in this one, with kind of a cream and cinnamon colored granite." She talked about her plans for the rest of the house too, until she looked up and noticed they'd already reached the beach. Her cheeks warmed. "I'm sorry I'm chattering like a flock of gulls."

He touched the small of her back with one hand and motioned with the other for her to lead the way down the beach toward the area below her own house. "I like to hear you explain it. It's obviously something you love."

Something she loved. She looked over and watched him walk beside her across the sand. *This* was love, she suddenly realized. Yes, there were the feelings of love tripping through her pulse to the point she was almost dizzy with the high of it, but mostly it was the realization that for this man she would *choose* any number of things. She would choose self sacrifice; vulnerability; respect and honor. She would choose to face an uncertain future with him, if he would give her the opportunity to do so. And she would choose humility. She needed to apologize. Even if he wasn't here to take her back, she owed him that much.

She laced her fingers together. "Jalen, I—" The words died in her throat and her feet stumbled to a stop.

There before them on the beach out near the waterline was a rather large cement sculpture of words. The foundation word had been laid out flat on top of the sand. Even from here she could make out the letters, J-E-S-U-S. The foundation was broad and thick and buried partially in the sand. Atop it, Jalen had formed two other words separated by a heart—Jalen and Riley. These letters stood upright, perpendicular to the foundation of Jesus. The words Jalen and Riley were connected into the letters that formed Jesus.

Jalen stood quietly beside her, fingers draped over the front of his pockets. He glanced down at the sand he was digging at with the toe of his shoe, and then back up to meet her gaze. "I had everything I wanted to say all planned out, but none of it is coming to me right now." Consternation twitched his lips. "Just...you mentioned that you feared all relationships for you might be written in the sand. That one crash of a wave might wipe them out. And well, I wanted to show you that when a relationship is grounded in Jesus, no matter how big the waves are, the foundation stays strong."

Even as he said the words the first far-enough-reaching wave of the incoming tide overtook the sculpture. It washed over the base, rolling the sand into turmoil all around it, but the sculpture didn't budge.

"I can't promise you we won't have turmoil in our future, Riley. But I can promise you that if you give me a chance, I'll do my best to keep my feet on the foundation of Jesus, and my heart set on the choice of loving you."

A layer of moisture suddenly blurred her vision. "I was coming to find you this afternoon to apologize and ask you if you could forgive me for forgetting so easily the lesson God is trying to teach me about the fact that He wants to bring good into my life. I'm going to try and do better in the future, but I might mess up again. Just like I did this time." She scooped her hair back from her face in a frustrated gesture. "I'm so good at messing things up, Jalen. Even when I'm trying my hardest not to. I thought I was doing what God wanted me to by letting you go, and it turned out I was doing just the opposite by rejecting a good gift He was trying to give me in place of the ashes of my past relationships."

There was still a measure of pain in his eyes, but his brows had lifted on a bit of hope now. "So, you think you could learn to love me like I love you?"

She stepped swiftly over in front of him and touched the side of his face with one hand. The fact that she'd made him feel like he might be a man she could not love pained her more than any words thrust at her ever had. She could offer him nothing but the truth in that moment. "I already love you. And I want *us* so much it hurts, Jalen."

She felt his whole body relax, and he offered her a watery smile. "Are you willing to take one day at a time and face the future with me, then?"

She nibbled on her lower lip. Could she do this? Was this really the blessing that God had for her? *Bouquets of roses for your ashes.* The words whispered through her and brought so much relief, she lost the strength in her legs and leaned hard into Jalen. She nodded slowly.

A luminous joy sparkled in his eyes. "Good. Because even though I used eight long pieces of rebar to stake that sculpture into the sand, I was terrified it might still be moved by those incoming waves and ruin my analogy."

She laughed out loud. The sound expressing the pure joy that was pumping through her.

Jalen smiled for a brief moment, before he let his gaze roam over her face. "Seriously, I want to have the privilege of telling you every day how beautiful you are." He bent and dropped a kiss on a freckle on her nose. "That your freckles make me smile." He kissed first one eyelid and then the other. "That one look from your amazing eyes can all at once turn my knees to jelly and give me the strength to scale any mountain."

Pleasure, peace, and elation rippled through her. And it was the most natural thing in the world to lift her mouth to his and offer all of herself to him. No more holding back.

His lips captured hers and a sound escaped her. It was part sigh and part longing. But mostly it was full of thankfulness.

The love of this man that God had set aside just for her was only a shadow of the love God had for her. But for now, for this time on earth, it was more than enough.

Epilogue

Five Years Later

Riley planted her hands on the bathroom counter and stared down at the pregnancy test, her jaw still slack. Even though this was the fourth month in a row that she'd missed her cycle she hadn't dared to even consider hope. Her mind had certainly conjured up all sorts of scenarios from early menopause due to the internal damage, to more serious things like cancer.

But... tears welled in her eyes. *Roses for ashes.*

A banging on the bathroom door jolted her upright. "Mommer, I need to get in there before everyone arrives!"

Riley grinned. "Give me a minute, Cole."

Her mother, the Sumners, Cahills, and Teagues

were all coming to dinner tonight. And Cole—her and Jalen's thirteen-year-old foster son—had a major crush on Alyssa Cahill. She would have liked to linger in the ethereal moment, but Cole was right. With everyone arriving in less than an hour, she needed to get out of here and finalize the preparations, instead of staring deliriously at two pink lines on a stick.

She snatched up the wand and stuffed it into the cupboard under the sink where she could show it to Jalen later. Washing her hands, she studied the glow in her eyes in the mirror.

How was she going to keep this to herself until she could find a moment alone with Jalen tonight? She was so excited her hands were jittery.

She opened the door and Cole started to shoulder his way past her, but then he froze. "What?"

She raised her brows. "Hmm?"

"You're all smiley."

Riley ruffled a hand through his blond hair. "Just having a good day, I guess."

Cole ducked away from her touch. "Hey. Don't destroy the masterpiece." He hurried over to the mirror and angled his head this way and that, checking out his golden spikes.

Riley chuckled. "The masterpiece looks just fine. Have you seen Micah?"

Apparently satisfied with his hair, Cole dashed back past her. "Nope. Probably in his room still."

The other foster son they had living with them

was fifteen, and a lot more introverted than Cole. He spent a lot of time reading in his room. But Riley was so thankful for the way God was using her and Jalen in these boys' lives.

Only a couple months after they'd gotten married, she and Jalen had finalized the renovations to this house—the one she'd been remodeling in the Bluffs. They'd added a wing with a couple bedrooms and had greeted their first foster daughter six months later. Connie had been seventeen when she came to live with them and was now midway through her degree in nursing at Oregon State. After Connie, they'd taken in the two boys. Both of them had absent fathers, and mothers who were in jail for one reason or another. For the past few years, Micah and Cole had been permanent fixtures in their house and Riley loved them fiercely.

At first the kids had called her Mom R, short for Mom Rivera, but even that had gotten run together and now the boys just called her Mommer.

She paused before the window at the end of the hallway and stared past the green of the back lawn set with the picnic tables for tonight's get-together to the pacific beyond. One hand rose to touch her stomach.

How many times had that same gesture been one of hopelessness? But today... A thrill of joy tripped through her.

Downstairs, the doorbell rang.

Riley hurried to answer it. Her mom stood on the other side, holding a pasta salad, and looking regal and exquisite, like she always had in the years before Dad had stolen her self confidence.

"Hi Mom. So good to see you!" Riley pulled her into a firm embrace.

She was so thankful for the good changes God was bringing about in her mother's life. During her time in jail, she'd gotten plugged in with a wonderful chaplain who had regular Bible studies with the ladies. She'd come out a new woman. It thrilled Riley to no end to sit next to her mother at church each Sunday.

Beauty for ashes. God's promises to her continued to roll through the years.

Riley gestured Mom through the entryway. She would have loved to share her news with her right then, but Jalen would be the first to know. If she could ever get him to herself tonight.

"Have you heard from Rem?"

That was Riley's only disappointment about tonight. She'd hoped that he'd be able to get away from college and come home for the weekend, but he'd begged off, with the excuse that he needed to study. Riley had a feeling it had more to do with studying the sweet girl he'd been seeing, than educational subjects.

Mom carried the salad through the back slider and set it on the buffet table Riley had set up in the shade along one wall. "Oh you know, with him no news is good news, but I think he was actually going to Christina's home this weekend to meet her family."

"Oooohhh!" Riley cooed.

Mom smiled. "I'm so glad he's found such a lovely Christian young woman."

"Me too."

The bell rang again.

"I've got it!" Cole yelled.

Riley winked at her mother. "That must be the Cahills arriving."

Mom chuckled and followed her back into the house where they greeted Reece and Marie, Alyssa and four-year-old Davey, named after Reece's father. Alyssa looked ill at ease as Cole stared at her like she'd just hung the moon.

Riley nudged him. "Cole, I think Jalen just arrived with the tank of propane. Why don't you go out and help him set up the grill."

"But..."

"Now, please."

With a sigh, he slumped off to do her bidding.

Alyssa eased out a breath. Marie suppressed a grin and tossed Riley a wink, while Reece clung tightly to Davey's hand. Marie had often described her son as a rocket in tennis shoes. The boy never stopped moving. Even now he was squirming and doing his best to escape his father's firm grip.

Micah appeared at the bottom of the stairs and Riley saw a solution to Mr. Rocket's dilemma, at least for the moment. "Micah, would you mind taking Davey out to the trampoline?"

Micah's face lit up. If there was one thing that could make that boy come to life, it was the vibrancy of a child. Riley fully expected him to become a teacher after he graduated in a few years.

Taysia and Kylen arrived just then and Riley bent to smile at six-year-old Zoe. "Micah is just taking Davey out to the trampoline, would you like to go too?"

"Yes!" Zoe bounced up and down like a rubber ball and spun in a circle. "Can I, Dad?"

Kylen took one look at his very pregnant wife and nodded his agreement.

"I'll go with them." Alyssa looked hopefully at her mother.

Marie nodded. "That's fine."

Riley's heart broke a little for poor Cole. He had such a crush on Alyssa, but she couldn't see anyone but Micah when she was here, and Micah seemed oblivious to the whole situation.

Micah took both children by their hands and led them out to the back yard, Alyssa on his heels.

"Someone will bring the twins as soon as they get here?" Riley called to Micah, making her tone more of a question than a statement, and Micah gave her a smile and a thumbs-up.

Taysia handed Mom the pan of brownies she'd brought, and pressed one hand to her lower back. "I swear this baby gets heavier by the hour."

Riley chuckled and tipped a nod toward the backyard. "I set up a reclining lounge chair just for you. As soon as Justus and Dakota and the boys get here, we can eat. Everything is just about ready. So please have a seat and just rest."

"You put her into a recliner and we might never get her out of it," Kylen teased his wife. She smacked him a good one and waddled her way across the living room toward the back yard.

As if on cue, the Teagues stepped into the entryway.

"Is this where the party's at?" Justus asked, one eighteen-month-old twin on each arm.

"Oh my goodness they're huge!" Riley tickled two little roly-poly bellies. "I haven't seen them for two weeks and they've both grown an inch!"

"And added ten pounds," Dakota said dryly. She was balancing a side dish in each hand, and had a blue diaper bag draped over one shoulder.

The twins, River and Brooks, were the spitting image of their father, right down to their striking blue eyes.

Riley motioned Justus toward the back yard. "Micah and Alyssa have all the kiddos corralled at the trampoline if you'd like to give the dynamic duo to them, as well."

Mom had been busy transporting all the dishes each family brought to the buffet table outside, and now she took the two bowls from Dakota. Lucia bustled by, laden down with other salads she'd had prepared in the fridge. "Everything is ready, Miss Riley."

Riley smiled. No matter how many times she'd tried to tell Lucia she could drop the *Miss* now, Lucia stubbornly insisted on sticking with the name she'd called her by since she was a newborn just home from the hospital.

Riley wondered how Jalen was doing at the grill. But just then Cole poked his head through the back slider. "Mommer! Pops says to tell you he's ready whenever you are."

"Thank you, Cole. Tell him we're coming." Riley motioned everyone out to the backyard. "I guess the food is on, y'all. Please just find any seat you want, and as soon as Jalen has prayed, it's first-come-first-served at the buffet table."

Riley followed all the people she loved most in the world out to her backyard. They all gathered around, and Jalen stepped up behind her and wrapped his arms around her. She leaned contentedly against his chest and nestled her head against his shoulder.

"Alright everyone. Let's say a prayer," Jalen called.

The stubble on Jalen's jaw scuffed her cheek as he thanked the Lord for his abundant blessing in food and friends.

As soon as he'd said amen, there was a mad dash of children scrambling to be the first in line, and adults clambering to hold them back and trying to instill some manners.

Jalen started after Cole, who had finagled his way to the front of the line, but Riley saw their only moment of solitude for the rest of the evening slipping away, and grabbed his hand.

A furrow formed on his brow as he looked back at her, their hands stretched between them.

"What?"

She tipped a nod toward the still open slider just next to them. She let all the love she was feeling for him in that moment be an invitation in her eyes. "I have to tell you something."

The furrow in his brow deepened. "What did Cole do now?"

She only chuckled and led him into the living room. She stepped right in front of him until their toes were touching. Leisurely, she draped her arms around his neck, and then pressed their foreheads together.

He was looking at her like she might have fallen just a little off her rocker.

"Jalen Rivera, God just keeps showing me how good life can be when we simply step off of our sandy foundations onto the foundation of *Him* and live our lives for His glory."

Jalen kissed her softly. "We serve an awesome God, Ri." He said the words but she could still see a hint of curiosity on his face. He was wondering why she'd brought him inside to tell him that, just now.

"Yes. We do." Her throat closed off and she didn't know if she would be able to choke out the happy news.

He swayed with her gently. "As much as I'd rather stay here with you, I don't think we should leave our guests on their own with Cole." Humor glinted in his gaze.

Riley chuckled but held on tight when he started to head back outside.

He gave her a questioning look.

She forced the words past the lump in her throat. "I'm pregnant, Jay."

He blinked.

She felt her ecstasy bloom on her face, and she nodded her assurance. "I'll need to go to the doctor to verify, but I think I'm at least four months along."

Jalen whooped. Then, laughing out loud like a crazy man, he swung her around in circles.

"What the heck is going on in here?" Cole stood in the doorway, holding a plate that was in grave danger of tipping all its contents onto the carpet at his feet. He licked some sauce from one thumb, eyeing them with raised brows.

Jalen gave Riley a quick wink. Their temples were pressed together as they eyed their God-given son.

"Mommer is expecting a baby," Jalen said, his arms tightening around her a bit as he did so.

Cole looked baffled. "Is that all? Wow. I thought the Seahawks game was on or something." Cole turned and clomped back out the door calling a loud reassurance, "Don't worry everyone, Mommer is just expecting a baby."

"What?!" three female voices called in unison.

And then the backyard seemed to explode with joy and congratulations.

www.ingramcontent.com/pod-product-compliance
Lightning Source LLC
Chambersburg PA
CBHW032226050726

47591CB00001B/283